ghosts just want to have fun

Vella Day

Erotic Reads Publishing

A Voodoo and Vampire Mystery
A Witch's Cove Whodunit
Book 3

Copyright © 2022 Vella Day

www.velladay.com

velladayauthor@gmail.com

Cover Art by Jaycee DeLorenzo

Edited by Rebecca Cartee

Published in the United States of America

E-book ISBN: 978-1-951430-52-8

Print book ISBN: 978-1-951430-53-5

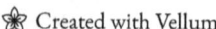 Created with Vellum

chapter
one

"I CAN'T BELIEVE it's time for you to go." I pressed my lips into a pout.

My cousin, Glinda Goodall, hugged me. "Jaxson and I won't be gone *that* long."

"I hope not, but a week seems like forever." Though, if the weather didn't cooperate, they might return sooner. I still didn't understand why they decided to go camping and hiking in North Carolina since Glinda disliked all forms of exercise, and climbing mountains would be a lot of work. "Have you ever hung a bear bag, pumped water, or started a fire?"

"That's what my fiancé is for." Glinda looked up at Jaxson and grinned.

"I told her that I'm expecting her to help. Glinda can pump the water and maybe cook."

I swallowed a laugh. I'd love to be a fly on that tree, watching Glinda navigate the out of doors. Jaxson was the one who loved traipsing around in the woods, and I trusted him completely to keep her safe. But camping? I worried she would be miserable. "I hope you have a fabulous time."

"I plan to." Glinda looked over at Iggy, her talking pink iguana familiar. "And you, mister, better behave and do what

Rihanna tells you to do. No flowers for a month if she says you sassed her or snuck out when you weren't supposed to."

The iguana lifted his head. "How is that fair?"

Glinda stood up straighter. "Are you saying you'd prefer to go camping with us instead of being cooped up here?"

My cousin had warned Iggy about the possibility of a bear sighting, not to mention how the nights could dip into the thirties or forties in the mountains. Temperatures that cold might kill the little cold-blooded reptile.

"No. Just go." He turned around and waddled under the sofa, his favorite hiding place.

Just as they were about to leave, someone knocked on the Pink Iguana Sleuths' office door.

"That must be Nicky." I thought she was stopping by in an hour. Either I misunderstood her, or Nicky had the time wrong. I voted for the latter. Keeping an accurate calendar wasn't Nicky's strong point.

"Who's Nicky?" Jaxson asked, sounding quite protective.

"Nicky Andrews and I are in the same photo class together, and we have a class project to do. We're going to work on that today."

Glinda smiled. "I think that's wonderful."

I pulled open the door and motioned her in. Nicky entered and then stopped. "Oh. I thought you said your cousin was on vacation."

"They're just leaving." I introduced them.

Iggy came out from under the sofa. "Hi, I'm Iggy."

Nicky looked over at him. "Iggy, Rihanna has told me all about you. Nice to meet you."

"You can hear me?"

She grinned. "Yes. I have witch powers. Rihanna didn't mention that?"

"No. She doesn't tell me anything." With that announcement, he turned around and went back to his hiding place.

Nicky chuckled. "You did say he was sassy."

"He is at that," I threw back.

"Don't mind my familiar," Glinda said. "He's mad because we are going camping up North, and he can't go. It's too cold and probably too dangerous for him."

"Well, don't worry. Rihanna and I will take good care of him."

Really? I thought she was only planning to stay for an afternoon.

"Thank you." Glinda hugged me again, and then she and Jaxson finally headed out.

"Have fun!" I called.

Once they were gone, I motioned for Nicky to take a seat. "So where do you want to take pictures?"

The assignment was all things vintage—as in old.

"Well, I've been doing a little reconnaissance of the area. A couple of miles from here is an abandoned farm house that would be wonderful to photograph."

Since I'd only moved to Witch's Cove, Florida two and a half years ago, I wasn't familiar with every nook and cranny of the area. "Sounds perfect. Let me grab my camera."

After I stuffed a few bottles of water in my backpack, I bent down to find Iggy. "Do you want to come with us?"

He slowly crawled out. "Do you have food for me?"

Iggy was always hungry. "I can pack a container of lettuce, but we'll be outside, so there's always leaves for you to munch on, you know."

"Yeah, but I like lettuce better."

"I'll pack some for you then." I guess that meant he wanted to join us, though I wasn't sure why he wanted to go. Maybe he was a little out of sorts now that Glinda and Jaxson were gone.

It wasn't as if he couldn't come and go as he pleased, if he stayed here, however. There was a cat door he used all the time, and he had no shortage of friends he could visit. Some were of the animal variety while others were gargoyle shifters.

I placed a few pieces of lettuce in a container that I jammed into my backpack. I looked over at Nicky. "Do you mind carrying Iggy?"

"Not at all."

She picked him up and let him ride on top of her pack. When he didn't complain, we took off. I drove while Nicky navigated since she had seen the place from the road and knew where we were going—more or less.

After following her directions for a while, Nicky pointed to a poorly paved road. I made a right turn and had to hold the wheel tightly to avoid being bumped all over the place.

"Hey, watch it," Iggy said, clearly not happy with the road conditions.

"I have no control over the ruts in the road."

"You could drive slower."

Smart aleck. I did let up on the gas a little.

Nicky picked him up and held him, which would be more secure.

"It's over there," she said, sounding excited that she found the location again.

I slowed. "It sure looks abandoned, what with the roof half caved in."

No one seemed to be about either. Good. We certainly didn't need to be questioned by the sheriff should someone see us and call it in, though Steve Rocker knew Glinda and me very well. Worst case, he'd tell me not to enter a property without permission in the future.

I cut the engine, grabbed my pack from the back seat, and slid out. The day was really warm, but thankfully there was a slight breeze to keep us from overheating.

Since the property wasn't fenced, it made for easy access to the house. The best part was that the nearest neighbor was a football field away. I didn't see any cars in their drive, and from the lack of care, the homestead might be empty too.

Nicky lifted her foot. "I wasn't thinking when I dressed this morning. I didn't wear the right shoes for this excursion."

The grass hadn't been cut in a long time, and since Nicky had on backless sandals, it would make walking around a little difficult. At least I had worn sneakers. "How about we start by taking pictures from the street?"

"Good idea."

"What about me?" Iggy asked.

"What about you? Do you want to wander on your own?" No one was about, so Iggy couldn't get into too much trouble, assuming he didn't mind forging through the weeds. "I hope there are no snakes in the grass."

He lifted his head. "How about I ride on the top of your backpack? It will be safer up there."

I smiled. "Sure." I lifted Iggy from Nicky's pack, though he would have been safe with her too.

After a few initial shots of the front, I walked left and Nicky headed right. It was always fun to compare the different photos at day's end. I then traipsed down the side of the property where the grass was matted down, as it would be easier to walk there.

"Someone's in the rear of the house," Iggy announced. "Maybe we should leave."

I squinted but saw no one. "Where do you see someone?"

"I told you. In the house. I have eagle eyes, remember? Or should I say, lizard eyes."

Iggy could see and hear better than I could. "Are you sure it's a person though? No one should be in there. The house is missing half the roof, and most of the windows are broken."

"It's a person, but he's not moving."

That was strange. "I'll check it out when I get over there."

"Hurry." Iggy crawled up the strap of the backpack and sat

on my shoulder, making it hard for me to lift my arm to take any pictures. He might be a lot of things, but he wasn't this demanding without a reason—at least not usually.

"Fine. Which window is it?"

"The back one."

I wanted to move closer to the structure anyway, and this was a good excuse to do so.

I called out to Nicky, who walked over to my side of the house and waved. "Find something?"

"Iggy said he sees something inside." I motioned that I was going in, and Nicky held up a hand, implying she was happy where she was.

As I waded through the grass and around the overgrown shrubs, I had to step around beer bottles, rocks, paper products, and a host of other unsavory items. I had the sense this place might have been used as a hangout for the teenage crowd.

Okay, technically I was a teenager since I was only nineteen, but I'd had to grow up faster than most once my dad died. I take that back—once my alcoholic mother told me at the age of three that my father was dead. Truth was, he was an undercover FBI agent who didn't want the world to know we existed for fear someone would harm us. Regardless of the reason, it was just me and my mom, though I was lucky enough to meet my dad last year—right before he was murdered.

As long as I'm spilling my guts here, I might as well introduce myself. I'm Rihanna Samuels. I moved into the back room of my cousin Glinda's office when Mom went into rehab. And the rest is history as they say, other than the fact I have a real hunky boyfriend, Gavin Sanchez, who's away at college studying to be a doctor.

Iggy lifted his claw as if to point. "Do you see him?"

My heart stilled. A very stiff looking man was sitting

upright in a chair, appearing quite dead. "Oh, my. Maybe it's a mannequin."

Iggy sniffed. "Nope. He's dead. You know how much I hate the smell of death. When Glinda or you visit the morgue, you come back reeking. And I can smell real good, remember?"

Yes, he could, though I smelled nothing. The odor could be mold coming from inside the abandoned house. "Let's see if we can get inside."

"Are you kidding? Leave me out here."

I glanced at the lizard on my shoulder. "I need someone to protect me."

And yes, I was kidding.

"Then contact Hugo."

Excluding Iggy's immediate human family, Hugo was Iggy's best friend. The gargoyle shifter might be mute, but he had a lot of powers. Teleporting was just one of his abilities, as was temporarily paralyzing someone with a touch. "I don't think a dead man can harm me."

Iggy lifted his claw to his snout, which was his version of a face plant. "The person who killed the guy could still be in the house."

I lifted him off my shoulder so I could see him better. "Why do you think he was murdered?"

Iggy opened his mouth and then shut it.

"I thought so," I shot back. "Come on."

If I believed we were in any kind of danger, I would have contacted Hugo. I stopped, letting reason sink in. At the very least, it might be smart to let someone know where we were in case we didn't return.

Since Genevieve, another gargoyle shifter, was Hugo's girl-friend, I called her. Hugo, being mute, didn't do well using a phone.

She answered right away. "Hey, did Glinda and Jaxson leave?"

"Yes, about a half hour ago. I just wanted to let you know that my friend Nicky and I are at an abandoned farm house on the outskirts of town taking pictures. Iggy spotted what I think is a dead guy inside."

"Oh, no. Where are you exactly?"

I didn't want to bother Genevieve, but she, too, could teleport, so I told her the approximate location.

"We'll be right there."

I didn't have the chance to even say she didn't need to come when both Hugo and Genevieve showed up. I swear she must have secretly implanted a GPS chip under my skin since she and Hugo always could find me.

"You came!" Iggy shouted.

Hugo smiled and removed Iggy from my grasp. Those two had such a special bond.

"Where is this guy?" she asked.

I guess her sense of smell wasn't as good as Iggy's either. "In the rear of the house."

The three of them disappeared. Now that those two had arrived, it was probably safer inside than out.

Nicky picked her way over to me. "Who were you talking to just now?"

I explained about the two teleporting shifters. Because Nicky was a witch, she seemed to take their existence in stride. I had to say, she did better than I did when I had first met those two. Changing from an animal into a human almost seemed normal to me, but stone to flesh? That was a totally different thing.

"Hugo and Genevieve are checking out the inside to make sure it's safe."

"From the roof collapsing?"

I guess I forgot to mention the real reason for their sudden appearance. "No, from the dead guy inside—or someone who might have killed him. That's assuming it's not a very lifelike mannequin. Though if it were, Genevieve and Hugo would have come out and told me by now."

"Oh, my. Did you call the sheriff?"

In my surprise at seeing the body, I'd completely forgotten the protocol. Considering my boyfriend's mother was the town's medical examiner, I should have remembered. "I'll do that now."

It seemed strange even to me that I had the sheriff's office on speed dial, but I did.

Pearl Dillsmith, the sheriff's aging grandmother and dispatcher, answered. "Witch's Cove sheriff's department. How can I help you?"

She usually recognized my cell phone number. Pearl must have been distracted. "Hey, Pearl, it's Rihanna. I'm afraid I found a dead body—or, I should have said, Iggy did."

chapter
two

"A DEAD BODY? I thought Glinda took care of those," she chuckled.

I could see why Pearl thought I was kidding. "Yes, a *real* dead body. Both Genevieve and Hugo are with him now. I haven't gone in to look though, so I can't tell you much."

"Oh, you're serious, aren't you?"

"Deadly." I inwardly smiled at my own pun. I told her our location the best I could.

"I'll let Steve know."

"Thank you."

Since I had performed my civic duty, I might as well go inside, even though the smell could be bad. From a photographic perspective, I had a feeling the inside would be even more interesting than the outside. Taking some crime scene photos wouldn't hurt either.

I waved my camera. "Let's check out the body and pretend we're crime scene unit photographers."

"Really?" Nicky's lips pulled back into a grimace. Since she wasn't trying to block her thoughts, I could read them quite easily. She didn't want to be anywhere near death. Nicky had told me how she'd watched her grandmother die a few months ago, so I could understand her hesitancy.

"Better yet. Why don't you wait for Steve?"

Nicky nodded. "I'll do that."

As I headed to the back, I carefully stepped over some fallen pieces of rotten wood that I assumed had come from the roof. The back door thankfully wasn't locked, not that one of the shifters couldn't have opened the door for me if it had been.

The first thing I noticed was the lack of dead body smell. The area was moldy and damp as I'd suspected, and the cloying scent made my nose wrinkle. If I hadn't been looking at the guy, I wouldn't have known someone had died in there. It was possible, he passed away a long time ago, and the odor had dissipated. However, if that were the case, why did his skin look so good?

I stepped over to Hugo, Iggy, and Genevieve. "Any idea what happened to him?" I didn't know why I asked since I couldn't imagine they'd know.

"He looks scared," Iggy said.

"Why do you say that?"

"His eyes are open."

"That happens sometimes when people die." Since Steve would be here shortly, I quickly snapped some pictures. "No one touched the body, did they?"

"No. Why would we?" Genevieve asked.

"Maybe you wanted to see if it was a real person and not some leftover Halloween dummy."

I took a few close-up shots, and after a quick perusal, I didn't see anything to indicate he'd been murdered. There was no bashing in of his skull or any bullet holes that I could see. Considering poisons often didn't leave any external evidence, he could have died that way. Or, he could have died of a heart attack or some other natural cause, despite being fairly young.

While Gavin had talked a lot about the dead since it was his mom's profession, he never mentioned a body being so stiff. Then again, I was no expert on what rigor mortis looked like exactly.

"He must have died recently, poor guy," I said.

Genevieve leaned closer. "Probably. His skin still looks flesh colored."

"I noticed that too."

Sirens sounded in the background. Less than five minutes later, Sheriff Steve Rocker and Gavin's mom, Dr. Elissa Sanchez, came in with two of her staff, along with a crime scene guy dressed in a suit of white.

I nodded to Gavin's mom, and then we all stepped back. Now wasn't the time to socialize.

While Elissa did her preliminary examination, Steve motioned me off to the side. "What were you doing here?"

Thankfully, he didn't sound mad. "Nicky and I had a photo assignment to take pictures of something vintage, and she came up with this place. Don't worry. We left the body as we found him."

"Did you spot anyone hanging around?"

If I had, I would have mentioned it when I called it in. I did live with Glinda, the queen of amateur sleuths, after all. "No. It was Iggy who saw this guy sitting in the chair."

"Did you check his pockets?"

I couldn't help but dip my chin. "No one touched the body."

It looked like Steve was trying to swallow a smile. "You're well trained. Thank you." He nodded to my camera. "Take any good shots?"

"I was in the middle of photographing the scene when you arrived."

"Send me what you have."

I wasn't sure what good that would do since one of Elissa's

men, as well as the dude in white, was snapping away. "Sure. I can't help but wonder who the guy is, and what he was doing here." I hoped Steve knew him.

"I'd like to know that too."

I guess that was his way of saying that was all he'd tell me —assuming he knew the deceased.

Steve glanced to the door and nodded. I could take a hint. This was a crime scene, which meant we needed to leave. I motioned with a lift of my chin to Genevieve, Hugo, and Iggy, that it was time to go.

Hugo handed me Iggy. Even though Steve had witnessed Genevieve and Hugo teleport at will numerous times, the rest of the staff had not. I was pleased that both gargoyle shifters waited until they were out of sight before disappearing.

Nicky was waiting for me outside. "Tell me everything," she said.

"The guy is dead," Iggy said. "What else is there to know? And the sheriff didn't say who it was, though I don't think he knew."

I looked over at him. "Was Nicky talking to you?"

"No, but you would have been long-winded."

I was not long-winded. "You have me mistaken for Genevieve or one of my two ghostly friends."

"Oh, yeah. Maybe."

When we reached my car, we slipped in, and I faced Nicky. "Are you okay?"

"Sure." She looked out the window and then turned back to me. "How dead was he?"

"What kind of question is that?"

"I guess I want to know if the person was murdered. I've heard so much about how your cousin solves all these crimes, and I thought it might be fun to try my hand at it."

I had no idea that Nicky was interested in something like

that. "Whether he died of natural causes or was murdered, dead is dead."

Nicky tilted her head. "You know what I mean."

Not really. "I don't know how he died, if that's what you're asking. Nothing was obvious. If you want, since Glinda and Jaxson are not here, we can do a little investigation. Usually, Steve asks for Glinda's help if he thinks magic is involved, though I'm not saying this case involves it."

"Cool."

Iggy crawled onto Nicky's leg. "I think you might be in luck."

"Why is that, Iggy?" Nicky asked.

"Because there was something odd about his death."

I had thought that also, but my imagination could get the best of me sometimes. "Why's that?" I asked.

"He looked almost alive."

"I think it's because he wasn't slumped over, Iggy. It's called rigor mortis. I'm guessing he died recently." So what if I had little to no expertise in the field? It sounded good.

"I know what rigor is. Sheesh. I can't help but hear a lot of what you and Gavin talk about."

Okay, that was creepy. "Are you eavesdropping on us?"

"No, but when you sit in the office and talk, I can't help but hear you discuss dead body stuff—and other gooey things," Iggy said.

"Well, my boyfriend is studying to be a doctor."

"Whatever. What do you think that dead guy would say about how he kicked the bucket?" Iggy asked.

"When Bella showed up as a ghost after she was murdered, she had no clue what happened to her. Are you saying we should call upon this guy and ask him, thinking he might be different?" Glinda's mom could usually converse with the dead, but the dead weren't always receptive to talking with us.

Iggy looked back at Nicky. "Have you ever seen a ghost? Rihanna and I have. Lots of times."

"Iggy, I wouldn't say a lot." Though, I spent a total of two weeks with Bella Benoit who'd been my cabin mate on a cruise until she was murdered. That's when she returned as a ghost. Her dying caused Lorenzo Bambini, a dead vampire, to visit. Phew. That case nearly did me in.

"Twice," Nicky announced.

That was encouraging. "Did you summon them, or did they just show up?" I had told her all about Bella and Lorenzo.

"They were summoned."

Iggy placed a foot on my leg. Since I was driving, I didn't look down at him. "Yes?"

"We should do a séance and ask the guy what happened."

He forgot one major thing. "Who should we ask for? Do you know his name?"

"No, but I bet Hugo can spy on the sheriff. He'll tell us the dead man's name when Steve learns who he is."

"That has potential." When we returned to the office, I cut the engine and faced Nicky. "I have a picture of the guy's face. Maybe someone in town knows him."

She grinned. "I like how you just went into sleuth mode."

"I guess I did. Since we'll probably have to wait not only for the autopsy results but on Steve to do some investigation, we need to find another place to take pictures. But first, how about I feed Iggy, and then we can grab something to eat?"

"Perfect, and we can ask if anyone knows this guy," Nicky said. "Afterward, what do you say we check out an antique store and shoot some pictures of the items?"

That sounded quite dull. "Or we can head to the docks and take pictures of some old boats."

"I like that idea better."

We escorted Iggy upstairs. Once I fed him, Nicky and I headed out to the Spellbound Diner, which was run by Dolly

Andrews, a woman who had her finger on the pulse of the town. I swear she knew almost everyone in Witch's Cove. And if she didn't know them, she often knew someone who might.

Since I put the dead man's age around forty, Dolly was our best bet to have known him since she was the youngest of the fairly old gossip queens.

"Do you think she'll really be able to identify this man?" Nicky asked.

"Maybe. She's best friends with Pearl, the sheriff's dispatcher, who happens to be his grandmother. When Steve learns something, Pearl finds out and tells her girlfriends."

Nicky smiled. "I like it."

Nicky lived closer to the college than she did to Witch's Cove, so she didn't know our gossip queens.

We entered the diner, and I immediately headed to the back where I usually sat. Dolly spotted me, but because she was with a customer, she merely waved. I hoped she'd come over after she finished with him.

We both grabbed menus and checked out the offerings. Since I ate there a lot, I only checked to see if Dolly had any specials. Today, she didn't.

Nicky studied the menu and then put it down. "I think Iggy has a point."

"About what?"

"When we find out the man's name, we should try contacting him."

"I'm game," I said.

Dolly finished serving the man at the counter and came over. "Hey. Did Glinda and Jaxson get off okay?"

I smiled. The whole town seemed to know my cousin's vacation plans. "They did."

"How long will they be gone?"

"She claims a week, but I'm betting Glinda will grow

weary of hiking and the lack of a shower and suggest they return before then."

Dolly smiled. "I hear you." She looked over at Nicky. "You're new."

I explained that Nicky and I went to school together. "Guess what? We were on a photo shoot today when we found a dead body."

Dolly's brows pinched. "For real?"

She seemed quite excited. Dolly loved hearing gossip, especially if she learned some juicy tidbit before Pearl or the other gossip queens did. To be honest, I was surprised Pearl hadn't already called her good friend and mentioned the deceased.

"Yes." I pulled out my camera. "This might be a bit maudlin, but I took a picture of him. I'm hoping you might know him."

As soon as I turned the camera toward her, she lifted it up and studied the image. Her eyes widened, and her cheeks sagged. "Oh, no."

"You know him?"

"Yes. He was a Witch's Cove star when he was in the band."

"What band? And who is he—or, rather, who was he?"

"His name is Gabe Rebel."

Since I didn't grow up here, I had no idea who that was, though I had the sense that wasn't his real name. "What was the name of the band?"

"The Rebels. Gabe was their lead singer." She swooned. "Back in the day, they were really popular, and Gabe had every woman after him."

I pulled out my phone and typed in his name. "Is that his real name?"

Dolly waved a hand. "Oh, no. His real name was Gabriel Rebenel, but he shortened it to Rebel."

"How old was he?" Nicky asked.

Dolly glanced at the ceiling. "Let me see. I'd just opened the diner when he was hitting his stride. That was thirteen years ago. So I'm guessing he'd be in his late thirties."

Nailed it. I looked at the photo again. His lifeless eyes took away from his good looks, but I guess he could be considered hot for an old guy. "You said he was in a band. I'm assuming The Rebels are no longer together?"

"No, they are, just not with the original members. Once Gabe left, their popularity waned. They still do concerts, but with a different lead singer. I lost track of them a few years ago. You might want to ask his former girlfriend, Kitty Fox."

Kitty Fox? "Is that her real name?"

"I don't know. I think Maude or Miriam might know more."

I grinned. "I appreciate it."

"So what can I get you girls?"

chapter
three

ONCE WE TOLD Dolly what we wanted to eat, I waited until she headed back to the kitchen to place our order before I said anything to Nicky. "What are you doing for the next few days?"

It would be nice to have someone around that I could bounce ideas off of. I was willing to admit that having both Bella and Lorenzo had helped me a lot with the last two cases, one of which was solving Bella's murder. As ghosts, they could go anywhere in a second and listen in on conversations. Believe it or not, their suggestions regarding who had the best motive for murder was often spot on.

Nicky shrugged. "Nothing much. I only have one class on Tuesday and one on Wednesday. Why?" Her eyebrows rose.

"If you're serious about checking out the dead guy, do you want to hang out for a few days?"

Nicky clapped. "I'd love to. That would be so cool."

I mentally did a fist pump too. "We do have to be careful if —and that's a big if—Gabe Rebel was murdered. People don't like snoops."

Nicky did a mock shiver. "What about that big friend of Iggy's? Didn't you say he could protect us?"

"Hugo can, for sure, but let's do some digging first. We haven't learned if Gabe was killed yet."

"Good idea. What about Gavin's mom? If she's the medical examiner, won't she be able to tell what happened to Gabe?"

"Probably, but she can't tell me. It's a confidentiality thing."

"Got it," Nicky said.

Another server carried over our order, and we dove into our meal. "Don't fill up. We'll have to hit either the tea shop or the coffee shop to learn about Kitty Fox."

"Understood. I can see that this job could be hard on the body." She patted her flat stomach.

"It's why I usually only order a tea and not a pastry when I visit establishments that have homemade desserts. Glinda, however, indulges every chance she gets. She loves to take advantage of the twin sisters' baking skills."

"The twin sisters?"

"I keep forgetting you don't live in Witch's Cove. Maude Daniels runs the Moon Bay Tea Shop whereas her twin, Miriam, owns the Bubbling Cauldron Coffee Shop, which is across the street."

Nicky sighed. "Maybe I should move to Witch's Cove. It's nicer than where I live."

"It is a great place."

Since we had people to talk with, we ate quickly. As a thank you to Nicky for being willing to help, I paid.

"Let's try the tea shop first. It's closer," I said.

"You're the boss."

Hardly. It was only a five-minute walk to reach the store. Thankfully, the place wasn't overly crowded. Because I liked to see the comings and goings of the town, I opted to sit by the window. It was where Glinda liked to sit too.

Maude smiled and nodded at us. As soon as she finished at the cash register, she came over.

"I heard you found *someone*." Maude looked around, probably wondering if talking about a dead body would hurt her business. Why I didn't know. She blabbed to Glinda all the time about my cousin's murder cases.

"I did." I motioned she take a seat. I didn't know why Pearl would have called Maude and not Dolly. "Did Pearl tell you the person's name?"

Not that I didn't believe Dolly, but it would be nice to have some confirmation.

"Sure did. Dolly called Pearl a minute ago, and she called me and said it was Gabe Rebel."

Ah, so that explained the line of gossip. "What do you know about him?"

Her lips pressed together. "He was an amazing musician and lead singer."

If he and his group were that good, I'm kind of surprised I hadn't heard of them before. "Dolly said he quit the band quite a while ago."

"Yes. Rumor has it that his band members were a little wild, partying way too much and such, and Gabe decided that wasn't the life for him anymore."

"How did the band take losing their main guy?"

She shook her head. "Not well. I don't remember their names anymore, but you should talk to Kitty Fox. She and Gabe dated for a while. She can give you the lowdown."

Yes! I was hoping she'd bring up Kitty's name. "Do you know where I can find her?"

Maude looked off to the side. "I think she lives in Liberty. You could ask Steve to find out about her."

Steve Rocker's fiancée was the sheriff over in Liberty. If anyone could find her, Misty Willows could. "Thanks. Do you know what happened to Gabe after he left the band? He was too young to have retired."

"I believe he works—or, should I say, worked—as an independent financial advisor. Gabe rarely stopped in here, so I didn't follow his career."

"I appreciate the input."

Since Maude had a business to run, she pushed back her chair and stood. "What can I get you two?"

I ordered my usual tea, and Nicky asked for a coffee and a scone.

Maude smiled. "Coming right up."

Once she left, Nicky leaned over. "Maybe a band member wanted the band to reunite, and when Gabe said no, they killed him."

I chuckled. "How would a dead band member help them reunite?"

"Hmm. Good point. As you can tell, I'm new at this."

I smiled. "We're both new at this, though tossing out ideas, no matter how crazy they might sound, can often lead to answers. The band still performs. If Gabe decided he wanted to return to singing, it could be a problem for the current lead singer who might not want Gabe to take his place." I wiggled my eyebrows.

"You think the lead singer might have killed Gabe?" Nicky's voice escalated.

"Shh." I couldn't help but read her thoughts. Nicky seemed to be in awe of this whole sleuthing thing. "No. I was making that up, though it's possible. Like I said before, we need confirmation that the man was even murdered."

"Gotcha. He might have been young, but young people die of natural causes. He could have been born with a heart defect or something."

I liked that Nicky didn't limit herself to the obvious. "Exactly."

"So what's next? If your medical examiner is prohibited from telling you how he died, how do we find out?"

A server carried over our food. "Elissa will eventually give her report to the sheriff. However he died, we'll find out soon enough. The gossip in this town is insanely fast." I sipped my drink. "If Elissa has nothing to do today, I'm thinking she'll check out Gabe. If the cause of death is obvious, we'll know quickly. If not, it could take her days."

"Bummer. How about after we finish our snack, we head to the docks to take our pictures for the photo assignment? No telling when we'll have time later on, especially if we find out someone killed the guy."

She was really getting into it. "I love that idea. Taking pictures often clears my head."

"Me too."

I continued to sip my tea while Nicky delved into her coffee and scone.

*

Nicky and I spent the next few hours shooting all sorts of cool boats at the docks. We were particularly interested in the ones in dry dock since they were usually in a state of disrepair, which made for the perfect vintage shots.

By five, we decided it was time to head back to the office and compare photos.

"Do you think the medical examiner will be finished yet?" Nicky asked.

"Probably not. But as soon as I learn anything, I will call you. Okay?"

"Perfect."

We switched cameras and scrolled through each other's photos. Since we had to turn in ten images, I picked my favorite ones of hers, and she picked her favorites of mine. Not that we'd agree, but it was nice to have someone else look at them.

Nicky stood and collected her gear. "Where's Iggy?"

"Iggy?" I called. When he didn't answer, I figured he was either with Hugo or with Aimee, my aunt's talking cat. "He's out socializing with someone. He'll come wandering in when he feels like it." I just hoped he hadn't gotten himself into any trouble. While Tippy, the seagull hadn't bothered him of late, it was always possible Iggy might decide it would be fun to taunt him.

Nicky hugged me goodbye. "Tomorrow then. Call me."

"I will."

Once she left, I headed to my room to work on the photos. We were only allowed to change the contrast on the pictures and nothing more.

When I finished, I dragged out Glinda's whiteboard. This was her way of figuring out how to solve her crimes—not that we knew a crime had been committed yet. Unfortunately, I couldn't list any suspects, but I could make a to-do list.

For starters, I wanted to find out the name of The Rebels' band members, and then I would ask Misty Willows if she knew where Kitty Fox lived. Of course, I would only impose on Misty if Gabe hadn't died of natural causes.

I leaned back against the headboard. I wish Jaxson were here. He was so good at investigating people. However, like most teens, I rocked at social media.

Between me, Nicky, and Iggy, I bet we could do a séance to see if Gabe would appear and give us a clue about what happened during his final moments alive. If not, I could ask if Bella, one of my ghost friends, would be willing to scour the *other side* for him. I really wished I knew how that worked. Even when the last ghost explained what happened in the afterlife, I was still unclear about most of it.

Before I tried to contact Gabe, however, I wanted to learn

about those involved in this case. Social media was often a font of information. I went over to my desk, opened my laptop, and checked out a few sites for something about the band and this Kitty Fox.

I found one of the band's social media sites, which included a picture of them. There were four members: Rod Anderson, Steely Coutreau, DMan, and Sev Little. When I read about each of them, they seemed like nice guys. There wasn't much discussion about the group when Gabe was a member, but I saw they had a gig coming up in Tampa this weekend—a show I just might have to go to.

I glanced to the ceiling. "Bella or Lorenzo, if you guys can hear me, I sure could use your help." I chuckled. Like I could just ask and they'd show up? Okay, I was hoping a little bit.

Iggy came into the room. "I'm back."

"What were you doing?"

"Nothing."

That didn't sound good. "Did you see Hugo or Aimee?"

"No, Bandit and I were hanging out."

Bandit was also a familiar, but unlike Iggy, he was a raccoon. I sniffed. "Since you don't smell, I take it you weren't looking in any garbage cans?"

"I'm so over those days of diving into those stinky messes."

I smiled. "I'm glad."

"Did you find out anything about the dead guy?"

"Not much." Mostly to help me get my thoughts in order, I told Iggy everything we'd learned.

"I bet Jaxson or Glinda could find out stuff."

Ouch. That hurt. "I'm sure they could, but they aren't here."

"Did you try to contact Gabe like I suggested?" Iggy lifted his head in a challenging pose.

"I will as soon as I find out if he was murdered."

Someone knocked on the office door, and I slid off the bed. "Any idea who that is?"

"How would I know? My friends just teleport in here."

"True." Stepping past him, I went to the door, but before I could reach it in time, Elissa, who was the medical examiner and my boyfriend's mother, entered as the sign instructed. "Rihanna."

Dread flowed through me. "Is Gavin okay?"

She waved a hand. "Oh, yes. I came about the body you found."

Relief filled me, though I would have thought she would have told Steve her results before me. Unless… I tried not to smile. "You don't know the cause of death, do you?"

"I have my suspicions."

"Do you think it might have something to do with magic?"

Her brows pinched. "I thought Gavin said you tried not to read a person's mind."

I chuckled. "I didn't read your mind. It seemed to be the only reason why you'd be here—professionally speaking, that is. Want to sit?"

"Sure."

After I fixed Gavin's mom and myself a sweet tea, she explained what she'd found. "Please note that our conversation is strictly confidential."

Iggy wandered in. "I won't say a word."

Good thing Elissa couldn't hear Iggy even though her son now could, thanks to a spell a local coven member had put on him.

"Of course," I answered.

"I can't go into detail, but I have placed his time of death about three to four days ago. Because of how you found the body, I could be off by a day or two. A lot of indicators are contradicting each other."

"Is the problem that you've never seen a body stay in rigor for so long?" Hey, I almost sounded like I knew what I was talking about.

She pointed a finger at me. "Not in this heat I haven't, which leads me to think magic might have been involved. I opened him up, but found nothing to indicate his cause of death. I sent his tissue samples to the lab and hope that will reveal something, like poison. I put a rush on the order. While I wait, I thought Glinda's magic necklace could help."

I sucked in a breath. "Glinda is in North Carolina camping and won't be back for a week."

She nodded. "I know, but I was hoping you could give it a try."

I'd never even touched my cousin's magic necklace. "I'm sure she wouldn't mind, but both Glinda and I always assumed that our grandmother had put a spell on the necklace that only Glinda could unlock."

"Steve told me that, but Glinda said she wasn't sure if you couldn't use it too. Can you give it a try? I've seen Glinda do it numerous times, and I can guide you."

"I suppose it can't do any harm." I looked over at Iggy, though I doubted he'd have an opinion. "What do you think?"

"Why ask me? It's not my necklace, but if you go, promise you'll shower when you get back?"

I smiled. "Promise."

chapter
four

"SLOWLY SWING the necklace back and forth over the man's feet and then work your way upward," Elissa said. "I'll pay attention to the pink diamond to see if it changes color."

I'd watched Glinda do this a few times, so I knew what to do—more or less. Glinda had told me what each of the colors meant, which helped. "I hope it changes color."

"If not, then either magic isn't involved, or the necklace doesn't work for you. We have nothing to lose in trying."

Even if Elissa hadn't been my boyfriend's mother, I would have given it a shot. Truth be told, it was kind of exciting to do this.

I continued to swing the necklace back and forth from his feet up to his abdomen, and when nothing happened, I sighed.

"You're doing great," Elissa urged. She must have seen how the tension in my hands had caused me to clutch the necklace.

Keeping my movement even, I continued to work my way up his body. I expected to see the stone change color around his heart, but it didn't. By the time I reached the top of his head, I huffed. "I guess the necklace isn't working for me."

Elissa nodded. "It was worth the try."

"What's the longest time a body has remained in rigor?" This guy seemed to be at the peak of stiffness when we found him.

"Considering he was in that hot house, I'd say two to three days. In that time, a body should have started to decompose."

"If he died before that, it makes sense to think magic was involved."

Elissa nodded. "I might just be overlooking something. I appreciate you trying to help though."

"No problem."

I removed my gown and gloves and left. Elissa had driven me to the morgue, but I told her I wanted to walk back.

Since Gabe Rebel's death supposedly happened days ago, and he was still in rigor, I was going to assume he was murdered by some magical person. So what if the necklace didn't prove it. My vampire ghost friend, Lorenzo, had told me that when a non-immortal vampire died, a witch would put a spell on him to keep his body from changing in case someone decided to bring him back to life. That meant magic *could* keep a body from decomposing. However, unless Gabe was a vampire, something else might be at stake—pun intended. But what?

As soon as I entered our office, I headed straight to the shower. And no, I didn't see Iggy. Good thing too. He would not have been pleased being around me.

After I cleaned up, I sent my photos of the crime scene to Steve. I was quite disappointed that they didn't show anything special in the images, but he might find something useful in them.

With that promise fulfilled, I decided to call Gavin. I'd had a stressful day and needed to chat with him. I grabbed a quick snack before retreating to my room, logged into my video chat, and called him.

He answered on the second ring. Gavin was on his bed

surrounded by books. "Hey, what's up?" he asked, sounding happy that I'd called.

"Did your mom talk to you today?"

"No, why?"

I explained about finding a dead body. "Your mother thinks magic might have been involved."

"You do know you shouldn't be discussing anything she tells you, even with me, right?"

I chuckled. "You're her son. Who would you tell?"

His eyes widened. "Are you kidding? I'd have my fellow biology students glued to their seats if I told them the things I've seen."

I adored Gavin. "I'm sure you can keep a secret."

"I can. What are you going to do next?" Gavin understood I had to follow through on this. It was in my nature.

"Tomorrow, I'm going to see if I can contact the deceased."

"More ghosts?" I nodded. "You know if you keep contacting them, they'll soon be swarming you."

I hadn't thought of that. "I hope not. I plan to see if maybe Bella and Lorenzo can help." Gavin had met them—and seen them.

"Good idea. Promise me one thing."

"What?"

"If you decide to look for the killer—assuming Gabe was murdered—take Hugo with you. I couldn't sleep at night if I thought you were in danger."

I blew him a kiss. "I promise."

Someone knocked on his dorm room. "That's Craig. We're studying together for our upcoming test."

"Okay. I won't keep you." After telling him that I loved him, we disconnected.

Even though I spent every night alone in this office, I could feel Glinda and Jaxson's absence, as strange as that sounded. Since I couldn't do anything more tonight, I grabbed my e-reader and settled down for a nice evening of romance.

*

The next morning, because I wanted to see if Aunt Fern—another gossip source—had learned anything about Gabe's death, I headed over to the Tiki Hut Grill for some breakfast —with Iggy, of course.

He loved Aunt Fern, and if he wasn't chatting with her, he always enjoyed tormenting her cat, Aimee.

When I entered the restaurant, the place was fairly crowded, for which I was pleased. Aunt Fern was at the counter helping a customer check out. She looked up, smiled, and motioned I sit at whatever table I wanted. Before I did, I carried over Iggy and placed him on the counter.

The customer stared at him for a moment and then quickly left.

"Hi, Aunt Fern. Long time no see," Iggy said.

"Oh, my sweet boy. It's been too long."

"I'll let you two catch up. I'm in dire need of coffee. Iggy, how about filling Aunt Fern in on the murder?" I said.

She sucked in a breath. "I heard about Gabe Rebel's death. It was such a shock and a loss to our community."

I hadn't considered she might have known him. "What can you tell me about him?" Coffee could wait—barely.

No one needed to check out at the moment, so I could bend her ear for a bit.

"Have you ever listened to the band?" she asked.

"I can't say that I have. I did look them up, but I didn't focus on what they played."

Aunt Fern sighed. "Their music was wonderful and so soulful. Gabe had the most beautiful voice."

"So they were good?" I didn't know why I asked since she'd just said how amazing they were—or at least how good Gabe was.

"They used to be. 'Call Me' was the song that took them to the top of the charts. The Rebels toured for a few years and did very well—until Gabe decided to quit."

"Because the group was into too much partying?" I was going off what Maude had said.

"I think so. His girlfriend at the time, Kitty Fox, would know more."

Iggy faced me. "We need to spy on her."

"Oh, really. Are your volunteering?" I asked.

"No, but Hugo can do it."

"So, Detective Iggy, do you know where Kitty works or where she lives?" Misty Willows might be able to find out, but I didn't want to bother her if I could help it.

He flipped around and faced Aunt Fern. "Can you find out?"

She smiled. "I'll see what I can do, young man."

Another customer came up to the counter to check out. "Let me know what you learn, okay?" I asked.

"Sure."

I picked up Iggy. "Do you want to visit Aimee?"

"For a little bit, and when I'm done, I'll go back to the office."

"Okay, but don't stay too long. Nicky and I need you to help with a séance."

"Really?"

"Yes, really."

"I won't be long then. Can you walk me to the staircase?"

Sometimes, he could act quite entitled. "Sure."

I carried him past the kitchen to the back of the restaurant where Glinda's apartment was located. She lived on the second floor across from Aunt Fern's place. Glinda had installed a cat/iguana access in both doors a while ago so Iggy could come and go as he pleased, as well as visit Aimee. I placed him on the banister and watched him crawl up it. I stayed for a moment to make sure he reached the top, though I didn't know why I bothered since iguanas were born climbers.

Now it was time to eat—and have that much-needed caffeine fix. I hadn't seen Glinda's friend Penny waitressing, so it didn't matter where I sat. I found a random open table and looked over the menu.

Once I decided, my mind wandered to poor Gabe. I'd love to find out how the band responded to Gabe's decision to leave. I couldn't imagine they'd be happy. After all, he had been their money-making star—at least I assumed he was—since he was the lead singer. But would they have a reason to want to kill Gabe after so many years? Hopefully, Gabe would know.

Often times Glinda would write down questions she wanted to ask the dead, so I would do that too. Unless, of course, Gabe was like Bella and Lorenzo and could stay around for days at a time once he was summoned.

The server came over, poured me some coffee, and took my order. While I waited, I called Nicky, who hopefully was awake.

"Hey, Rihanna." She sounded a little groggy. Whoops.

"Are you up for a little séance?"

"Are you kidding? Of course, I am. When?"

"When you get here."

"I need to clean up and then grab something to eat, but that I can meet you at the office in an say an hour?"

"Perfect. See you then," I said.

My breakfast arrived shortly, and I gobbled down the food. As always, it was delicious. When I was done, I paid Aunt Fern who naturally fussed, saying it was on the house.

"I'm going to get Iggy. Nicky, my friend from school, and

I are going to try to contact Gabe. Are you free to help, by any chance?"

Aunt Fern placed a hand on her chest. "I wish I could, but I need to be here. Tell Gabe that I think he is wonderful."

That wasn't something I'd ever seen Glinda do, but if there was time, I'd bring it up. "Sure."

I went upstairs and knocked on Aunt Fern's door. Naturally, neither Aimee nor Iggy could open it. "Iggy, we need to go. Nicky is coming over shortly," I called out. "I need your help."

A minute later, he pushed open the cat door. "I thought I had time."

I shrugged. "Plans changed, but no problem. I'll ask Wendy to help with the séance instead." That was Glinda's mom.

"No. I can go."

I smiled, picked him up, and headed back to the office.

By the time I set up the coffee table with the candles, Nicky arrived, and she was bubbling with excitement.

"How many times has a séance worked for you?" she asked me.

I wanted to be honest. "Glinda usually does the séances, or Gertrude Poole. She's our Witch's Cove psychic. But I would say the ghost *usually* appears, though not always. And when he or she does, they only stay for maybe thirty seconds."

"That's disappointing, but let's hope we get lucky."

I motioned she sit down, and then I placed Iggy on the table. "We need to keep our eyes closed and our fingers—or claws as the case may be—touching. Is that how you've done it?"

"Yes."

I tried not to chuckle. Nicky hadn't been involved in a séance in a long time—assuming I was reading her mind correctly.

I lit the candles. "Ready?"

"Yes," Nicky said.

Iggy knew what to do. He was a veteran. The three of us connected our hands. "I'm trying to reach Gabe Rebel or Gabriel Rebenel. We found you in a broken-down farm house. I don't know what happened, but I'm sorry. We'd love to help find out how you died."

I was nervous. The person who tried to contact the dead was usually the one with the most experience, though I supposed between the three of us, I was the most qualified. Good thing Iggy usually cheated and opened his eyes if he sensed a ghost, so if Gabe appeared, Iggy would let me know.

After a good minute of waiting, my patience ran out. I opened my eyes and broke contact. "That was a bust. I'm sorry."

Nicky pressed her lips together. "You tried."

"You might as well ask Glinda's mom to talk to him," Iggy said. "Hopefully, she won't fail."

"I probably will ask her." I was about to blow out the candles when I had another idea. "Before I give up, are you two willing to give it another try?"

"Why?" Iggy asked. "He's not coming."

"I know, but I want to see if maybe Bella can join us. Maybe she'll have better luck finding Gabe. She's found others who've passed."

Nicky nodded. "We're already here. Why not?"

"Great."

Once more we connected our hands, and then I called out to Bella Benoit. Since she'd visited me—unsolicited—about a month ago, I felt as if we had a shot at contacting her.

"We really need your help, Bella. Or Lorenzo Bambini. Or both!"

"Well, it's about time you called." That voice came from my former cabin mate, Bella Benoit, seconds later.

When I opened my eyes and saw both her and Lorenzo, I jumped up. "You came!"

"Of course, I did. I've spent the last few days listening to this guy bemoan the fact that he can't find his coffin, and I really needed a break. As a ghost, I just want to have fun, and coffin hunting is not high on my list of must-do activities."

I chuckled. That was so like Bella.

"Lorenzo, you still haven't found your coffin?" I didn't know why I asked. Bella said he hadn't.

Nicky cleared her throat. Whoops. I was so caught up in seeing them again, that I forgot about Iggy and Nicky.

"Can you see them?" I asked Nicky.

"Ah, yeah. I told you I've seen ghosts."

That was a relief.

Bella floated over to Iggy and tried to pick him up, but of course she failed.

"Hey. That was cold," he complained.

"Sorry, Iggy. I was just happy to see you. I forget sometimes that I died."

Lorenzo moved next to Bella. "For the record, I ran into Bella and asked her to help me look for my coffin. After two days, I said I wouldn't keep her." He faced Bella. "And I didn't moan or bemoan anything."

Oh, boy, it was fun to have them back.

chapter
five

"YOU SAID YOU NEEDED HELP?" Bella asked.

"Yes."

Between me, Nicky, and Iggy, we gave them the lowdown on Gabe Rebel. "Aunt Fern said she'd try to locate his former girlfriend. I'd like to find out if there were any hard feelings between Gabe and the band when he left."

"How can we be of service?" Lorenzo asked.

Not that I expected the vampire to look any different from when I saw him last month, but he and Bella were dressed in the same outfits they had on when they died. In Lorenzo's case, it was a tuxedo and a top hat.

"We thought Gabe, the guy who died, might be able to tell us what happened," I said.

"Meaning what?" he asked.

I thought the meaning was clear. "Can you two find him and bring him here? I'm not sure if that's how it works, but Bella, you found Lara and took her to the hotel room in Nebraska. Can you do that again with Gabe?"

Bella looked over at Lorenzo. "What do you think? Are you up for scouring the afterlife?"

He pretended to tap the wooden spike in his chest. "What

else do I have to do? Find a coffin? Oh, yeah. That's what I've been doing for the last forever number of days."

I refused to suggest that maybe whoever killed him didn't want Lorenzo to find his coffin. That implied this person was also a vampire. Of course, my vampire lore wasn't as up to speed as it should be.

Bella faced us. "We'll give it a go. What does he look like?"

I went into my room and grabbed my camera. After I pulled up the photo, I showed it to both of them.

"Ooh, he's kind of cute for an old guy." Bella was nineteen, too, so her comment didn't surprise me. It was possible she'd had a birthday since her murder, but I didn't think that counted.

"What are you waiting for?" Iggy said, and we all laughed.

Bella and Lorenzo disappeared.

"Whoa," Nicky said. "That was a trip."

"Tell me about it. After I found Bella dead in her bed, I didn't believe my eyes when she just appeared later that day."

"You probably thought your mind was playing tricks on you," Nicky said.

Iggy waddled over to her. "That's why she called me. Rihanna needed someone to confirm that what she saw was real."

I'd actually called Glinda, but Iggy happened to be there. "To my surprise, Glinda who normally can see ghosts, couldn't see either Bella or Lorenzo, but Iggy could."

"That's because I'm special," Iggy said with way too much arrogance.

Nicky held up a hand. "I don't know what to say."

"You don't need to say anything. Just know that these two are real real ghosts. Believe it or not, they are actually pretty good at sleuthing. I just wish I had a way to contact them whenever I wanted."

"You just did," she said.

"True. I should have said that I wish I could call out their names and have them appear."

"That would be sweet. If that was how easy it was, I'd have called for my grandmother to appear months ago."

Now I felt bad. Once more, I forgot that Nicky had recently lost her. "I think these two are pretty special."

"They must be," she said.

I explained that I'd found my father dead on the beach. "I've tried to contact him, but I guess he can't be reached." Or else he doesn't want to be reached for some reason.

Nicky nodded. "I get it."

As if my thoughts about the afterlife sparked something out there, three ghosts appeared, including Gabe Rebenel I had the sense that time wasn't the same in the afterlife as it was here.

I studied him. Poor guy. He looked somewhat stiff even in his ghostly form. How that was possible, I didn't know. Good thing his method of moving involved floating instead of walking.

"Gabe Rebel, I presume?" Of course it was, but I wanted to be polite and ask.

"Yeah. What's going on?" He looked around. "Wait a minute. Who are you?"

I wasn't surprised he had questions. "My name is Rihanna Samuels. This is my friend Nicky Andrews along with our talking iguana, Iggy. The three of us found you in an abandoned farm house on the outskirts of town."

Iggy waddled closer. "You look pretty good for a dead guy."

Gabe raised an arm, and when he planted his hand on his chest, it went into his body. "Whoa. I'm dead?" He looked at me and Nicky. "You guys found me?"

"We did." I wanted to know why he couldn't tell he had

died? If Elissa was right, Gabe had passed quite a few days ago. Bella had figured out she was a ghost rather quickly.

Bella shook her head. "At least I wasn't in denial."

She did it again. I swear Bella could read my mind, and here I was the mind reader.

Gabe looked confused, and I could understand why. "Yes, you are deceased. Do you know what happened?"

He stared at me for a moment. "If I didn't even know I had died, how could I know what happened?"

Gabe had a point. Kind of. If he thought about it, I bet he could figure out what occurred before he passed. "Let's start with why you were at that old farm house in the first place." Assuming someone didn't kill him and move his body there, thinking no one would ever find him.

His body seemed to relax. "It's a long story."

Nicky grinned. "I like long stories."

"Okay then." He looked down at his body, lifted his transparent hands and studied them. "That isn't good."

"You got that right," Iggy said. "I don't think you'll be playing the guitar any time soon."

Ouch. That wasn't nice to remind Gabe that he'd just lost everything.

"I guess not." Gabe's voice trailed off.

"Back to your really long story," Nicky urged.

"Oh, yeah. Well, it's kind of embarrassing. If you know I play the guitar, then you know I used to be in a band." We all nodded. "After I left the group, I started my own financial services business. Unfortunately, of late, the investments started to tank big time, and I became a bit depressed. That was when I decided it might be time to get back into performing."

"I invested some of the money my dad left me into the stock market, and my portfolio took a beating recently, so I understand," I said. "The market being in a slump was not your fault though."

"Yeah, well a few of my clients didn't see it that way. One of them was trying to have my security license revoked because one of my recommendations didn't pan out."

"Could one of them have killed you?" I asked.

"I wasn't murdered."

We all glanced at each other. "No? Then how did you die?"

Gabe floated across the room, looked out the window, and then returned. "I have no idea."

Bella moved next to him. "With time, things might become clearer. What was the last thing you do remember?"

"Ah...Oh, yeah. I was to meet DMan at that farm house—he's from the band I used to be in. I started writing songs again, and I wanted him to listen to one of them."

Nicky's mouth opened. "Do you have a lot more new songs?" she asked, sounding so hopeful.

Why hadn't I heard of his group before? I didn't live under a rock. Or did I?

"Quite a few," he said. "I thought they were some of the best ones I'd written, which was why I contacted DMan. After I left the band, he took over the job of setting up the gigs and stuff. He also played the guitar."

"Did he ask you to return to The Rebels?" I asked.

"Not exactly. He said he wanted to hear the songs first, and that if they were something the band might like to record, then he'd ask the rest of them if they were willing to take me back. Sev Little was my replacement. I doubt he'd appreciate me returning."

I wanted to pull out my phone and make a note of his name, but that might have been rude. I could always find him again on social media.

"Why would you meet this DMan at that dilapidated farm house? It was nasty," Nicky said.

He huffed out a laugh. "If you heard my lyrics, you'd understand. I wrote some intensely emotional songs, and I thought the farm house matched the mood. In case you didn't know, we usually recorded the songs in the studio but filmed them outside. We did it that way since the wind plays havoc with the sound quality."

That made sense. "You wanted to show this DMan guy where you thought you could shoot the music video, right?" I asked.

"Exactly."

"Did this gentleman friend show up?" Lorenzo asked.

"No."

"Who did show up?" I asked.

It was possible Gabe died of natural causes, and Elissa might have estimated his time of death incorrectly.

"No one."

That wasn't making any sense. "You were to meet DMan, yet he was a no-show, right?"

"Right."

The killer must have kept out of sight then. "How was your health?"

"Good. I mean, I might tie one on now and again, but for the most part, I ate healthy."

Everyone claimed they ate healthy, though his body did look fit. "Maybe your death has nothing to do with any of the band members, but instead with your unhappy clients. Can you tell us the names of those who might have been upset enough to want to kill you?"

He dipped his head. "You'll need to take notes."

"Give me a sec." Yes! I was hoping he'd say that. I rushed to my bedroom and grabbed my laptop. Once I returned, I motioned for Nicky to move over on the sofa so I'd have room to type. "Tell me."

"Let me give you some background first. About three months ago, I heard about this bio tech company that was about to go to the moon—or so everyone kept saying."

"Did you think one of their drugs would be approved by the FDA?" Bella asked.

Her question shocked me at first until I remembered her dad was a wealthy banker.

"Exactly. I had it on good authority it was *in the bag,* so to speak."

Oh, boy. So many people fell for things like that. "Who were these clients who lost a lot of money?"

"The ones who had the biggest losses were understandably the most upset. They were Mona Leanders, Arnie Driscoll, and Pamela Vetters."

I jotted down their names.

"Did they invest more than they could afford to lose?" Bella asked.

His brows furrowed. "You're just a kid. How do you know about that?"

"I am young, but my banker dad lectured me a lot—when he was home that was."

I was glad Gabe thought I was older, or he might not answer my questions. Probably because I was five feet nine that people added a few years to my age.

"I see." Gabe turned back to me. "The person who I never should have suggested it to is Mona; she put most of her life savings into this company. Her husband had recently died, and she really needed a windfall. I was sure this was the right thing for her."

"And when this company didn't receive the government approval, I assume the stock price went down?" I asked.

"Yes. Big time."

"You said Mona was upset. Did she threaten you?"

"She's seventy-two years old, so she wasn't a physical threat, but she said she planned to turn me into FINRA, the Financial Industry Regulatory Authority for deceiving her."

"You should have done her in," Iggy chimed in.

"Iggy. That would be murder."

"So? Someone murdered him."

"Why are you all so sure I was murdered?" Gabe asked.

"We aren't positive, but your body was found in a strange condition that implied it," I said.

"How so?"

"You were in full rigor mortis—and still are—which means—"

"I know what rigor means, but why do you think I was murdered?"

Glinda's magic necklace didn't prove he was, and his lab results hadn't come back, so I couldn't be sure. "There's no other explanation as to why your body didn't...decompose enough for you to get out of rigor. We think someone used magic to kill you." I didn't really understand it well enough to explain it properly.

If he hadn't been a ghost, and if he'd been drinking something, he would have sprayed all of us. "A witch did me in?"

"It could have been a warlock," Nicky said, trying to be helpful.

"Ah, can we say voodoo priestess?" Bella tossed in.

"You guys are crazy," Gabe said. "I'm out of here."

With that he disappeared.

chapter
six

"WHAT DID WE DO?" Nicky asked. "He was in the middle of telling us why his clients might have wanted to kill him. We can't help him if he doesn't help us."

"Perhaps I can talk some sense into him," Lorenzo said.

I held up my hand. "Lorenzo, how about you give him a moment to come to grips with all of this? If I'd just found out I'd died, it would upset me too."

"Rihanna is right. When I died on the ship, I was quite confused. I was lucky I had Rihanna to tell me what happened. Just knowing she was willing to help calmed me a lot."

Aww. Bella had never expressed her gratitude like that before. She really has mellowed with age. "Thank you."

Lorenzo floated to the ground and looked as if he was sitting. Whether that pose was more comfortable or not, I didn't know.

"I wish I could follow him to make sure he's okay." Lorenzo sounded sad.

That was so sweet. "Are you implying that a ghost could harm himself?"

Lorenzo tried to drag his hand down his chin, but as usual,

he failed. "I don't think so. But I would like to know where Gabe is. That is one downside of being a ghost who wants to follow another ghost."

"What's that?"

"He can see me. I'm not like Iggy's friend Hugo or his girl-friend in that they can cloak themselves to the point where they are invisible even to me."

I hadn't thought of that. "Gabe gave us the names of those troubled clients. Since they aren't dead maybe one of you can check them out."

"And the other one of us?" Bella asked.

"We need to see what the band members are saying about Gabe's death. Which of them is secretly happy he's dead and who is truly devastated?"

Before either could decide who would follow whom, my cell pinged. I retrieved it and checked the message. "Stay here for a moment. It's a text from Aunt Fern. I don't know how she did it, but she found Kitty Fox's work place."

Nicky whistled. "That's some gossip pipeline you have in Witch's Cove."

"I know, right?"

"Too bad I died on a ship. Rihanna, I bet if I'd been killed in your town, you would have solved the crime faster."

"I don't know about that."

"Enough talk. Let's get moving," Iggy said.

"Get moving to where?" I asked my cute little iguana friend.

"Ah, duh. We need to see if Kitty Fox is a witch or not. If she is, she might have killed Gabe."

That possibility hadn't occurred to me. "Why do you think she would have killed him?"

"Maybe she is still mad at him for breaking up the band," he said.

"Iggy, that was ten years ago, and the band is still together, albeit with a different lead singer."

The other ghosts nodded, indicating they agreed with me. "Then maybe she was mad that Gabe wanted to get back with the band but not with her."

Iggy usually had good insight. "You might be right." I looked over at the ghosts. "I know I said we should check out the band members and Gabe's clients, but I think it would be nice if Gabe was with us for that."

"I agree," Bella said. "Lorenzo and I will come with you to see this Kitty chick. I bet she knows the ins and outs of this Gabe guy."

"Because they dated?"

Bella tilted her head. "Sometimes I wonder if you were ever a teenager."

I chuckled. "I wonder about that too sometimes. Let's go. Iggy, how about if you go in Nicky's bag and do your yelling thing at Kitty to see if she can hear you."

"Roger that."

This should be good.

Since Kitty worked at a hair salon that was in Liberty, it took us about forty-five minutes to get there. While I didn't need anything done to my long hair, I suppose she could trim the ends. If Kitty was with a client, I would wait.

I drove and asked Nicky to use the GPS on her phone to direct us to the salon. I probably should have called Kitty's workplace to see if she was even there today, but I was willing to take my chances.

When we arrived, the parking lot was almost empty, giving me hope that if Kitty worked today, she might be free. When we entered, I inhaled the fruity smells of processed hair chemicals. There was something soothing about the hair dryers going and the scents permeating the air that helped relax me. Maybe I should have my hair done more often.

"Which one is Kitty?" Bella asked.

I hoped she realized that I would look like a loon if I answered.

"How may I help you?" the receptionist asked.

"I've heard Kitty Fox works here?"

The woman smiled. "She does. Kitty is in the back. I'll get her."

Once the receptionist left her station, I turned to Nicky pretending to talk to her. "Lorenzo, maybe you and Bella should find Gabe and tell him we are with Kitty. That might pique his interest in returning."

"Brilliant," Lorenzo said and then disappeared.

Bella shrugged and followed him.

"Can I help you?" someone asked.

I spun around to find a very attractive woman with auburn hair and a bit too much makeup for my taste. "Hi, I'm Rihanna. You came so highly recommended that I wanted to see what you can do for me."

She grinned. "Oh, my. Of course. Come with me."

Nicky looked down, probably embarrassed at my blatant lie, and walked over to the sitting area.

This would be a difficult conversation—one I could easily mess up, especially if Gabe showed up and started talking to me.

"What can I do for you today?" she asked.

"I need my split ends cut off." And no, I didn't need someone super talented to do that.

"Sure." Even though she sounded a bit disappointed, Kitty picked up her comb and separated one section of hair from another and pinned it to the top of my head.

When I studied Kitty, she seemed fairly calm. "I know this might not be a pleasant topic, but did you hear what happened to Gabe Rebel?"

"Gabe? No. What happened to him?" She instantly threw up a brain block. Darn.

I never could figure out how people did that, but thankfully not everyone could block their thoughts from me. "He was murdered a few days ago."

"Really? That's terrible." She kept combing my hair into sections and placing them on top of my head as if the news wasn't upsetting, despite her concerned-sounding words.

"It is. I heard you used to date him."

She waved the hand holding the comb. "For a little while. That was what? Nine years ago?"

"I'm new in town, but even I've heard of The Rebels." I didn't tell her I'd only heard of the band after I found his dead body.

"Everyone knows them. They were big back in the day, but they're just as good now."

Really? "Do you still keep up with them?"

"Sure. Sev Little and I are together."

That was a new twist. "Cool."

I would have asked if any of the band members were upset to hear about Gabe's death, but she wouldn't know since she'd just learned he'd passed—or so she claimed.

"Hey, Kitty, Kitty, Kitty." That was Iggy. I sure hoped he'd cloaked himself so no one could see him. Considering no one was shouting about seeing a pink iguana roaming about, I assumed he had.

Kitty, however, didn't respond to Iggy and even managed to keep her movements even.

"Guess she's not a witch," Iggy said.

Just because I'd never met a witch who couldn't hear a familiar didn't mean it wasn't possible. Iggy waddled back to Nicky, who might have no idea he'd even been out and about.

"Since Gabe Rebel died close to where I live, people

mentioned he'd written some new songs." I wasn't sure why I brought it up, but I wanted to see if she knew Gabe was trying to get back with the band.

"I had heard that, too, but I don't think anything came of it. Once he left, the band moved on. I doubt they'd want him back. Styles change, and it's been ten years. The group is more upbeat now. Gabe's music was bordering on melancholy."

I believe he called it intensely emotional.

Her fingers tugged on my scalp a little harder than necessary. Time to keep quiet.

"Kitty?"

Darn. I knew that voice—and it wasn't Iggy trying again to see if Kitty could hear him again. While I couldn't move my head much, when I looked in the mirror, I didn't see Gabe or any of the ghosts. Interesting. Maybe they didn't have a reflection.

"She can't hear you, dude," Bella said.

"Rihanna and Nicky could," Gabe shot back.

"That's because they are witches."

"Oh."

He should have figured out by the lack of screaming from the clientele that no one could see the three ghosts.

Bella had the sense to suggest Gabe move away from Kitty's station to give his former girlfriend a chance to work on my hair. Good thing too. She might have been faking it and had heard both him and Iggy.

Before Gabe moved to the other side of the salon, however, he tried to hug Kitty, but all he accomplished was to pass through her.

She shivered but didn't seem to understand what had really happened. Kitty probably chalked it up to the air conditioner turning on. Clearly, she had no idea a ghost was near.

Eventually, Kitty finished. Truth be told, I really had been in need of a trim. I thanked her sincerely, paid, and left.

Once we were in the car—and by *we*, I mean all five of us—Nicky faced me.

"So? What did Kitty say?" she asked.

"Nothing, other than she is currently dating Sev Little, one of the band members."

"That's hardly nothing."

"You're right."

"I heard she was with him, but he's a joke," Gabe said. "The guy can't even come close to staying on key."

"Do you think Sev feared you might say something about his poor singing if you returned?" I asked Gabe.

"I couldn't say. Other than having a drink with DMan a couple of times in the last year, I didn't interact with the band much after I left. I wanted to put the experience in the rearview mirror."

"If you didn't have much contact with them, maybe it wasn't one of them who killed you."

"You're probably right."

"Did you tell Kitty I'd died?" Gabe asked.

"Yes." If Gabe had hoped—when he was alive that was—of rekindling their relationship, it wasn't going to happen.

"Now that you've had time to think about it," Bella said, "who do you think killed you? Assuming you didn't just croak on your own."

"Nice choice of words, Bella." I chuckled.

"It's okay. I prefer the kidding to all this serious talk," Gabe said. "If I was killed, I'm leaning toward Arnie Driscoll. Don't men usually kill more than women?"

"Yes, but I don't think you were physically harmed."

"Then how did I die?"

"I wish I had all the answers. Like I said, the medical examiner thinks magic was involved."

He huffed. "What proof does he have?"

"Dr. Sanchez is a woman. She is leaning toward magic

because your body isn't...changing like it should." That was better than saying his body wasn't rotting. "When we return, I'll contact her to see if the status of your body has changed."

"That's creepy."

"You should go to the morgue and see that you're there," Bella said. "I did it, and it kind of gave me closure."

"Bella, that worked for you, but it might not be right for Gabe. Remember, you thought you had been thrown overboard, but trust me, I saw Gabe's body. He's there. And the medical examiner is completely honorable."

For the rest of the ride back to Witch's Cove, we remained silent. The only mind I could read was Nicky's, and she was quite overwhelmed, not that I blamed her. It wasn't every day a person was in the presence of three ghosts who chatted as if they were alive.

Once we arrived, Nicky, Iggy, the ghosts, and I went upstairs to the office. As soon as Nicky set her bag down, Iggy immediately crawled out. "That was a bust," he said.

"Not completely. We met Kitty," I said. "Just because she's not a witch doesn't mean she is innocent, though most likely she is."

"I agree. Oh, and don't forget to call your medical examiner lady to see if Gabe's body is still in rigor. We need to be certain that magic was involved," Nicky said.

"I'll do it now." I pulled out my phone and called Elissa. I was going to text, but why not call? If she wasn't free to chat, then I'd contact her another way.

"Rihanna, hi. Steve and I were just discussing the case."

That was interesting. "Cool. I wanted to see if Gabe's body was still in rigor."

Gabe and the other ghosts, who'd come in through the wall, moved closer.

"It is, which has me really stumped. I called a few of my fellow medical examiners for their opinion, but no one can explain it, especially since you found him in a hot, damp house."

"I take it I should look into the magic angle."

"Rihanna, this is Steve. You know Glinda would kill me if I let you investigate. Please let us take it from here."

"It's kind of hard not to investigate when both Bella, Lorenzo, and now the victim, Gabe, are here—in their ghost form, of course." Besides, unless he asked Genevieve and Hugo to help, I wasn't sure Steve could solve a case that involved magic.

"You said Gabe is there with you?"

"Yes."

"I know I can't see him, but I'd like to ask him some questions. Can you guys come over?"

It had taken Steve a while to believe me when I told him about Bella and Lorenzo in the first place. I think that when my boyfriend, Gavin, confirmed they existed, Steve was willing to believe me.

"We'll be right there."

chapter
seven

I DISCONNECTED and faced the group. "If you didn't hear, Steve wants to meet Gabe."

The ghost straightened. "Really? He'll be able to see and hear me?"

"No, and neither can the medical examiner, but I'll be there to translate."

Iggy lifted his head. "I can help."

"You know how you can help even more?" I asked.

"How?"

"Steve all but insisted that I have a bodyguard if I plan to snoop, which I do. Do you think you could give Hugo the lowdown and ask if he can help?"

"You bet!" Iggy scurried toward his cat door and left.

I was thrilled he felt included again. I stood. "Ready to be questioned, Gabe Rebel?"

"I guess so."

"We're coming too," Bella said.

"I didn't expect you to stay behind, but you might be of more use checking out this Sev guy, the lead singer of the band."

"Do you have a picture of him?" she asked.

The photo on the social media site was small. "How about we ask Steve for a photo if he has one and maybe an address—assuming he knows that Gabe was in a band. Then you and Lorenzo can check him out."

"I know where he lives," Gabe said, "but I'd have to show you. I never memorized his address."

"What about the poor woman whose husband died and then lost her invested funds?" Lorenzo asked. "Shouldn't we see how she is doing?"

"Mona Leanders. You can check her out, but I don't know what you'll hope to find," I said. "Her revenge was in attempting to have Gabe's license revoked."

"I agree with Rihanna," Gabe said. "Like I said, my money is on Arnie Driscoll, in part because I wasn't aware he'd borrowed the money from his brother to invest. Now there are two Driscolls who are unhappy with me."

"Do you know where they live?" I asked.

"Not off the top of my head. I would have to go back to the office and see what I can find."

I looked over at Nicky. "Gabe, since you can't open anything or turn on a computer, you'll need a human. You could have Nicky go with you once we finish speaking with the sheriff."

"That works."

"How will I get in? The office should be locked, right?" Nicky asked.

Gabe smiled. "Not to worry. There's a keypad."

With that settled, the five of us left and moved across the street to the sheriff's office.

Nicky and I went in, and of course, the others followed.

"Rihanna, this is a nice surprise," Pearl said.

I nodded. "Steve said he wanted to ask me a few questions."

"Sure, go on back. He's with Dr. Sanchez."

"Thanks." I was a bit surprised she didn't ask why Nicky was with me. Steve probably had told her that my friend had been with me when I found the body, and Pearl most likely assumed Nicky might have important information about the case.

When we entered his office, Steve's eyes widened a bit at Nicky being there, and then he raised his gaze and looked behind me. I had to assume he wanted to find out if he could see Gabe. After all, Steve could understand Iggy once I put a spell on him.

"You remember, Nicky?"

"Yes. Have a seat. Is Gabe here?" Steve asked.

"He is." I didn't mention that both Bella and Lorenzo were there too.

"Where is he?" Steve asked.

I didn't think that mattered, but I told him anyway. "He's next to me." I glanced in the correct direction.

"Gabe, do you know who killed you?" Steve asked.

Like I hadn't asked him that?

"Go ahead and give him the rundown. It might save time," Gabe said.

I told both of them about Gabe having made some poor stock suggestions to his clients, along with the three names of the most upset ones. "That was when he decided he wanted to return to performing with his band. Gabe was at the old house because he had some songs he wanted to share with DMan, one of the band members."

Steve took notes. "Were these songs on paper, on a flash drive, or what? I have no idea how these things are transmitted nowadays."

I looked over at Gabe. "It depends," he said. "I often use paper and pencil to get the rhyme schemes down but then transcribe them to the computer for speed, letting my muse flow. In this case, since I'd finished writing the song, I played them and recorded the music on my phone."

"I had no idea." I relayed what Gabe said.

"What did you have with you at the farm house?" Steve asked.

"Just my phone. The quality wasn't good, but I wanted to give DMan an idea of where my head was."

"He used his phone to record," I said. "I never saw it. Did you?"

Steve shook his head. "It's possible I missed it. The place was a mess. I'll see if Nash can look for Gabe's cell." Steve picked up the phone and called his deputy who hadn't been at his desk when we'd come in. Steve explained the situation. "No, that's okay. I can check it out. I'll be quicker." Steve disconnected.

"He's busy?" I asked.

"Yes."

"How about I ask if Bella and Lorenzo to look first? They can be there and back in a minute."

Steve's eyebrows rose. "Sure. Are they here now?"

"Yes." I nodded to my ghosts who quickly disappeared. "They can't move anything, so they might not be successful if it's hidden under the rubble."

"How about asking Genevieve then? She and Hugo have been to the farm house and know where Gabe was found," Steve said.

Bella and Lorenzo knew too. "Let's see what the two ghosts say first."

Sure enough the two returned in short order. "Due to our inability to look under some of the roof tiles that had fallen in, I changed into a butterfly and was able to spot something that appeared to be a phone," Lorenzo said.

I smiled. "You are ingenious, Lorenzo. Good job."

"I suggested he change into his animal form." Bella looked quite proud of herself.

"That was very smart of you."

Steve cleared his throat. "Well?"

I told him what they said. "I'll call Genevieve to see if she can retrieve Gabe's cell."

"Can you ask her to wear gloves? The killer's fingerprints might be on it."

"Let me have her come here first so you can give her instructions." I called Genevieve, and before I could thoroughly explain the situation, she arrived, though not in her visible form.

"Rihanna. Can we show ourselves with Elissa here?"

"Sure."

Hugo, with Iggy in his grasp, along with Genevieve became visible. Elissa's eyes widened. "Oh my."

I couldn't remember if she'd seen them teleport before. Oh, well. She had now.

I nodded to Steve who withdrew a set of rubber gloves from a package in his desk. "When you find the phone, can you wear these?"

"Sure." Genevieve took the proffered gloves.

"We can show them where it is," Bella said.

"Great," I said.

"It might be best if I remain here in case there are other questions I can help with," Lorenzo said.

I thought it odd that he didn't want to be with Bella. On the other hand, she could be quite over powering. "Excellent idea."

The four of them disappeared. I'm sure Iggy just wanted to go so he could be with his hero, Hugo. "Now, we wait," I said.

Steve turned back to where Gabe had been floating.

"Gabe, you mentioned the current lead singer, Sev, might not have been happy about you returning to the band?"

"It was a guess on my part. I planned to ask if I could be the lead singer again, knowing that Sev would probably be demoted to backup."

I relayed the information to Steve.

"What are their full names? I'd like to speak with them," the sheriff said.

Once more I relayed Gabe's answer. "Tell us more about these disgruntled clients of yours," I said.

That would take a while, but since he'd unceremoniously disappeared after he told us about Mona, I was interested in his take on the others.

"Tell your sheriff that Arnie Driscoll is an overachiever. He has no patience in that he wants to get rich quick."

"That's most people."

"Rihanna?" Steve asked.

"Oh, yeah." I relayed Gabe's comment.

"Was he the angry sort?" Steve asked.

"Impatient is a better word. Like I mentioned, I hadn't been aware he'd borrowed money from his brother. Using leverage in the market is highly risky. Don't get me wrong. It's great when the market rises, but catastrophic when the market goes down."

I told everything to Steve.

"That doesn't sound like a murderer to me, but I could be wrong," Steve said. "Gabe, did you warn them that all investments carried a risk?"

"Of course."

I nodded.

"I'd like to get their take on the series of events. Hopefully, I'll be able to tell if they had a strong desire to kill Gabe. What's the name of this bio tech company? I want them to know I have done my homework, so to speak," Steve said.

I think he really just wanted to convince them to trust him.

"It's called Cloud 9," Gabe said.

"Cloud 9," I repeated. Steve jotted it down.

Elissa leaned forward. "Gabe, did you ever have any blood disorder issues?"

"Not that I know of, why?"

I told her what he said.

"Your blood work showed some strange anomalies. In laymen's terms, your blood had extra ingredients not found in most people's blood."

He floated closer to her. "Like what?"

"Like what?" I asked, though repeating everything the ghosts said was becoming tedious.

"You had more stem cells and fewer white blood cells than most. No one I spoke with could explain it. Have you had any blood transfusions?"

"No, never."

I shook my head to indicate his answer.

Lorenzo cleared his throat. "Yes, Lorenzo?"

"I don't know what stem cells are, but I am aware that we vampires have decidedly different structure to our blood. Since I am more civilized than most, I drink my blood from a blood bank or from a deceased animal." He held up a wavy finger. "That made me think. Wouldn't the blood bank blood mix with my original blood? I imagine it would be very different from a person who has the same blood his whole life."

I hadn't thought of that. I explained what Lorenzo said to the medical examiner, though I wasn't sure what Lorenzo's experiences had to do with anything.

Elissa huffed out a laugh. "It's true that if a person has a blood transfusion, the two bloods mix. It's why most people have to be careful not to mix blood types."

"Lorenzo, are you thinking that Gabe could have been a vampire?" I asked.

"Possibly. His blood is different from regular humans, which implies he might be."

"You have to be kidding me," Gabe said. "I am not a vampire. That's completely ridiculous. Sure I might have bitten some kids as a child, but not after I grew up. And I never sucked blood. That would be disgusting."

I told them what Gabe said.

"Your parents never hinted that you might have been born different?" Elissa asked.

Gabe floated backward a bit. "I was adopted, so I don't know."

That opened up a whole new set of questions, though I wasn't sure it was relevant.

"Rihanna?" Elissa said.

I did the rinse and repeat session once more. "I admit I know little about vampires, so I have no opinion one way or the other if Gabe could be one or not."

"Ladies," Steve said. "While interesting, this isn't helping us point a finger at who wanted Gabe dead."

"If I may," Lorenzo said. "What if you are looking at this all wrong?"

"How so?" I held up a finger to Steve and Elissa.

"While I can tell if a person is a vampire or not, I'm not getting that vibe off of Gabe."

"See?" Gabe said. "I am not a vampire."

"My dear man. Don't be so hasty. I've known people who have fought the urge and won. You might be almost fully human, but you could have been born a vampire."

Gabe turned around and dragged a hand down his face. It was weird that I could see the motion through his body. He spun around. "You are all crazy."

"Just wait a second." I had an idea. "Lorenzo, would you say vampires are healthy individuals?"

"Oh, my yes. As I've stated before, we have superior strength and a built-in immunity that allows us to live for hundreds of years."

I relayed the conversation to Steve and Elissa up to that point. "How often did you go to the doctor?" I asked Gabe.

"Never. Okay, I went to the dentist, but that's all."

Which could mean he was a vampire—albeit one in remission?

"Oh, my. I think I might know what happened," Lorenzo said. "Or at least I have a possible explanation."

"Do tell."

chapter
eight

JUST AS LORENZO was about to tell us his theory regarding what might have happened to Gabe, our gargoyle shifters and Iggy returned. "We were successful," Genevieve announced, holding up the phone.

She placed Gabe's cell on Steve's desk and then removed her gloves.

"Was it hard to find?" Steve asked as he picked up the phone using another set of gloves before placing it in an evidence envelope.

"Bella showed us where to look. Like Lorenzo said, it was under some roofing material."

"Did you find anything else while you were there? I had our crime scene unit check the place, but you might have been luckier."

"No, but we saw animal tracks outside," she stated.

I didn't think that was relevant.

Steve's raised eyebrows implied he thought the same. "Thank you both. I appreciate your help."

Genevieve smiled and then turned to me. "Before we go, Iggy asked if Hugo could make sure you stay safe. Hugo said he would be happy to keep watch."

"Thank you." I didn't need an around the clock body-guard. "I'll call the next time I talk to someone who might be dangerous."

"Are you sure?" she asked.

"Yes."

"Okay." A second later, she and Hugo disappeared.

"What did I miss?" Iggy asked.

"Lorenzo has a theory about what might have happened to Gabe."

"God job, top hat man. Go ahead. Tell us."

I smiled at that nickname.

"I have heard of cases where a child is born to a vampire and a human. I know people think we vampires are the walking dead, but that isn't true since we do have children." Bella cleared her throat, and Lorenzo looked over at her. "Like I said, Bella, I have no proof that we are related, but that discussion is for another time."

I told the two non-magical people what was said—skipping the part about the fact that Lorenzo might be Bella's great-great-grandfather. I asked Iggy to be the interpreter to help things move quicker.

"You think I'm half vampire because my blood is different?" Gabe asked, though I wasn't sure who he was addressing.

Elissa looked over at Steve and then back at me. Iggy relayed what Gabe said.

"Gabe, I have no way of knowing. It's not like there is any literature on vampires. Rihanna, even you didn't know they existed until recently."

"That is true. For now, how about we leave Gabe's heritage as undecided."

"Thanks," he said as Elissa nodded.

I couldn't blame him for not being happy about it. He already had enough shocks to deal with.

"You haven't heard my theory," Lorenzo said.

"By all means. Go ahead and tell us."

"What if someone knew that Gabe was a vampire and did a stasis spell on him?"

Iggy told Steve and Elissa what Lorenzo said.

"What's a stasis spell?" Elissa asked.

"It's what was done to me." Lorenzo huffed out a breath, or tried to. "Rihanna, I thought I explained it to you. After I died, a very powerful witch and her coven put a spell on me to keep me young and vibrant during my death."

I smiled. "Oh, yes. That way when someone pulls that stake from your heart—your real heart—you will wake up and look as good as the day you died."

"Thank you for remembering."

I waited for Iggy to translate. He always liked playing an important part in this case.

"Not to put a hole in Lorenzo's theory," Steve said, "but I don't recall Gabe had a stake in his heart."

"Please tell your sheriff that I was merely mentioning what happened to me. As for Gabe, perhaps a sorcerer of some kind put him in stasis with the intent of bringing him back to life. That's all I meant."

Wow. I had to think about that. When Iggy had a hard time remembering everything Lorenzo said, I repeated it.

"Lorenzo is saying that someone might not have meant to harm Gabe?" Steve asked.

"That is what he's claiming. Mind you, it's a theory."

Elissa stilled. "If that is true, which I don't think it is, then I basically killed Gabe when I performed the autopsy."

I didn't want her to have any guilt over this. "No. Gabe was dead—at least to us. You did what you were trained to do."

"Great. I'm dead by mistake." Gabe turned around and moved to the far side of the office.

"Okay. I'll bite," Steve said. "What would prompt someone to put a body into stasis?"

No one said anything for a moment. Gabe turned around. "Could they have thought I was in danger and put me into this deadly trance thinking the person who wanted to harm me would go away once they realized I was no longer a threat?"

That was a lot of information in one sentence. While Iggy repeated it to Steve and Elissa, I looked over at Bella and Lorenzo hoping they could come up with a different option. "You guys have anything?"

"No," they said in unison.

Steve pushed back his chair and stood. "I think I need to speak with this DMan person. I'd like to know why he never showed up to speak with Gabe. Can you find out DMan's home address or where he might be now?"

"His real name is Dave Manford. He should be in the studio. How about I go with Steve and show him where it is?" Gabe suggested.

"Since he can't see or hear you, I'll have to go."

"I thought Gabe and I were going to pick up something from his office," Nicky chimed in.

I told Steve the information. I'd let him decide which should take precedence.

"Nicky, I think it would look a little odd if I walked in with both of you girls."

She nodded. "Fine. I'll take Iggy back to the office and wait there until Gabe returns."

She was a good sport. "I appreciate that."

"Should Lorenzo and I try to find Sev?" Bella asked.

"He's probably with DMan. How about coming with us? If he's there, you can see what he's up to."

"Okay."

Elissa stood too. "I'll double check the lab results, keeping in mind that Gabe might be a vampire."

"I am most definitely not a vampire." He nearly shouted it, but neither Elissa nor Steve could hear him.

Neither Iggy nor I repeated what he said as Lorenzo floated over to him. "It's not a bad gig. Being a vampire has its perks."

"Is that so? You're dead. I'm dead. Where's the fun in that?"

I was interested in Lorenzo's answer. At least there was a chance that someone could bring him back to life. I'm afraid there was no hope for Gabe. For that I was sorry. He seemed like a good guy, even if he wasn't a great financial advisor.

"Suit yourself," Lorenzo said. "At least some of the living care enough to find justice for your death." With that, he spun around. Go Lorenzo.

Gabe faced me. "I'm sorry. Lorenzo is right. I can't change what happened to me, so I will focus on helping everyone learn how I ended up dead."

I smiled. "I think you'll be happy you did."

Steve looked over at Iggy and raised his brows, clearly expecting Iggy to translate.

"I got nothing," the cute little iguana said.

Steve chuckled. "Traitor." He looked over at me. "Ready?"

"Yes."

Nicky picked up Iggy, and we followed Steve out with the other ghosts close behind. I was hoping that Lorenzo might be able to recognize if there was a real live vampire among the band members—or among Gabe's clients—who were trying to protect Gabe somehow. I realize Lorenzo's theory was far-fetched, but it was all we had at the moment.

Whether the plan was to protect or kill, it didn't really matter. The result was that Gabe was now dead. The problem was that if there was no physical evidence to show Gabe's cause of death, no court would arrest someone who we claimed put a spell on him. Even if we used Hugo to force a confession, a regular court would think the person was unstable at best.

My goal at the moment was to learn what happened. Punishment was a secondary concern

"Where is the studio?" I asked.

He gave me directions that I relayed to Steve. It took us about ten minutes to reach the strip mall where DMan might be working.

When Steve parked, he turned to me. "Let me ask the questions. Please."

Was I that pushy? "Sure."

"But do your best to see what the guy is thinking."

So that was what he wanted me for. "What if Gabe has a question? Can I ask it?"

"Do you think it's wise to let this band member know that Gabe is a ghost?"

"From experience, I find that people are less likely to lie if they believe a ghost is present."

"Then go for it." Steve pushed open his car door, and I exited too.

"DMan won't believe you if you say I'm here," Gabe said, sounding defeated.

I smiled. "You'd be surprised. Just think of something only the two of you could possibly know. There must be a detail that only you guys have shared."

"Oh, sure."

When we entered the recording studio, I sensed several of them were nervous that an officer of the law had entered. That was telling.

"I'm looking for DMan," Steve said.

The four men looked between them. "That's me," said the chubby man with the beard.

I glanced over at Gabe who nodded. When I didn't say anything, most likely Steve figured the guy was telling the truth. "Can we speak somewhere in private?"

"This about Gabe?"

"Yes."

Kitty must have called Sev and told him.

"Sure. Come into the back office."

Calling it an office was a stretch. I would have called it a hoarder's dream. Stuff was piled everywhere. And by stuff, I meant papers, disks—which I didn't think anyone used anymore—and a few musical instruments, as well as a laptop that was quite dusty.

DMan cleared off two chairs and tossed the contents on top of his already messy desk. We sat.

"How can I help you?" the band member asked, sounding quite sincere.

"When was the last time you spoke with Gabe?" Steve asked.

DMan blew out a breath. "I can't recall exactly. Maybe five or six days ago?"

"I didn't think Gabe was a member of the band," Steve said.

"He's not. Gabe left the band ten years ago when we were the most successful. I regret not convincing him to stay. We were young and stupid back then, and Gabe wanted something more. I couldn't blame him."

Gabe floated next to me. "I had no idea he felt like that."

DMan's mind was more or less open, and as far as I could tell, he was being honest.

"What was the nature of your last interaction?" Steve asked.

"He wanted to return to performing with the band. Gabe had written several songs that he was sure I'd love and said to meet him at some old farm house so he could play one or two for me."

"Only DMan never showed," Gabe said.

"Did you?" Steve asked. "Meet him, that is?

"No. The day I was to hear his songs, he sent me a text saying he had to cancel."

Gabe flew into DMan's face. "That's a lie. Tell the truth. You ghosted me." He huffed and then faced me. "That's irony for you."

Of course, DMan did not react since he couldn't hear or see Gabe. If DMan had been a warlock with ghost seeing capabilities, I doubt he could have avoided flinching at least.

"Can I see the text?" Steve asked.

That was smart.

"Sure." DMan retrieved his phone, pulled up the information, and handed it to Steve.

He read through the messages. "Mind if I forward these to myself? It will help with the timeline of Gabe's death."

"Sure."

Steve sent them. "Thanks. Did Gabe tell you what these songs were about? Or how many he had?" Steve asked.

"No, just that they were good."

"Rihanna, he is lying. I even sang a bit of one to him over the phone to give him the idea of the tone I was going for."

"Dave, are you sure Gabe never sang the song over the phone to you?" I asked.

"No, I swear I'd remember."

I saw no reason not to believe Gabe, but DMan seemed to be telling the truth too. My mind reading abilities must be off today.

"How did the other band members react to hearing that Gabe might want to rejoin the band?" Steve asked.

chapter
nine

DMAN SCRATCHED HIS BEARD. "They were okay with it."

"Are you sure?" I asked. Or was he afraid to say that Sev was angry because DMan didn't want to make his friend look guilty?

"Yeah, I'm sure."

Now was the time to pull the ghost-is-in-the-house card. "I know you will find this impossible, but Gabe's ghostly body is in the room with us."

As expected DMan laughed. "Sure he is."

"If you don't believe me, ask him a question that only Gabe would know the answer to."

"That's easy. What was the first song he wrote that was never published?"

"Really? That's all he's got. Tell him it was 'Whisky Blues'."

I relayed the answer, and as was usually the case, DMan looked flustered. Not to mention his mind was racing in an attempt to comprehend it.

DMan lifted his chin. "Maybe he told you."

DMan was looking right at me. "I never met Gabe, when he was alive, that is."

"You some kind of witch or something?"

"Yes, which is why I can see ghosts." I certainly wasn't going to reveal my real talent was reading minds.

"I don't know what Gabe is telling you, but it's a lie."

"Why would I lie? I want to find out the answers more than anyone."

Gabe had a point. "Let's get back to the band's reaction to Gabe wanting to return. Full disclosure, I just had my hair cut by Kitty Fox. She told me a few things."

DMan shook his head. "Kitty is a joke. She's only with Sev because she loves being a groupie."

Gabe leaned close enough to me that I could feel the chill. "That is true. I never did trust her."

Then why did he date her? I wonder if she might have been the one who wanted to harm Gabe—or was it possibly to save him? Now wasn't the time to bring that up, however.

"You're avoiding answering Rihanna's question. Who in the band wasn't thrilled with Gabe coming back?" Steve asked.

"You seem to know all the answers. Fine. It was Sev. He's the lead singer. If Gabe's songs were as good as he claimed, Gabe would have been our lead singer, putting Sev in the back-up position."

I didn't think we should focus on the obvious. "What about Rod Anderson or Steely Coutreau?"

DMan's eyes widened. What? I could use the Internet.

"They seemed happy with Gabe's return. We hit the charts when Gabe was in the band. Ever since he left, things haven't been wildly successful to say the least."

"That's why I felt guilty for leaving them in the lurch." Gabe leaned closer. "But I didn't want to be part of that lifestyle."

"I get it." I tried to keep my voice low, but apparently, I failed.

"What's he saying?" DMan asked. While he looked sincere, he was really laughing at me.

"That you're the one who killed him. He remembers that you went to the old house to see if it would be a good place to film, and you murdered him." I have no idea why I made that up, but I wanted to see his reaction. We weren't getting anywhere with the other line of questioning.

DMan jumped up. "You're crazy."

Okay, he might be telling the truth—not about me being crazy but about him not killing Gabe.

Both Lorenzo and Bella were laughing, clearly enjoying this farce.

Steve lifted a hand in an attempt to stop this line of questioning. He knew I'd stepped out of bounds. After all, this was an ongoing murder investigation that he was in charge of.

"Sorry," I said. "I wanted to see how you would react. I believe you didn't hurt Gabe."

"Thanks. I think."

"Do you think Gabe met with any of the other band members?" Steve asked.

DMan shrugged. "Not that I heard of."

"I'm going to listen in on what the others are saying," Bella said.

"I'll go with her," Lorenzo added.

I didn't mention their plan to anyone, in part because it might have messed even more with DMan's head.

"Now that Gabe has passed, if you had access to his music, could you use it?" Steve asked.

"Maybe."

"Care to clarify?" Steve asked.

"Gabe signed a contract when he left. We had a lot of jobs lined up, so when he quit, we had to cancel. That cost us money. The contract was Gabe's way of trying to make things right."

"Let me get this clear. Gabe signed a contract that said any future music belonged to the group?" Steve asked.

"Not exactly. It said we had the right of first refusal. We'd have to buy it from him. Now that he's dead, I guess that's out of the question."

"That's true," Gabe said.

Good to know. "But you said you never heard these new songs?" I asked.

"No."

Gabe moved in front of me. "Like I said, I played one of the songs for him. Too bad there would be no record of it."

"Do you have this contract?" I thought I sounded quite lawyer-like.

"Some place."

"I'd like a copy of it." Steve handed him a business card—a card I didn't even know existed. "Send it to me."

"Sure. No problem."

Steve excused DMan and asked that Sev come in. Before Sev arrived, I quickly told Steve that Gabe had said the contract was legitimate.

"Good to know," he said.

Sev came in, and Steve went through the same type of questions. Too often, Sev wasn't forthcoming, and Gabe confirmed Sev lied a few times.

"I didn't even know the guy that well. Why would he lie?" Gabe asked me.

I thought the answer was fairly obvious, but it wasn't like I could voice my answer in front of Sev.

Once Steve finished with the last of the band members, we piled into Steve's cruiser, only this time, I didn't see Bella or Lorenzo. It was smart of them to hang back and listen in on the discussion once the law left.

"What did you think?" Steve asked.

I assumed he was talking to me. "I think DMan was on the up and up even though his version of things didn't match up with what Gabe said.

"Can you be specific?" he asked.

"Gabe said he sang a song to DMan, I guess to convince him to meet."

"That's right," Gabe said.

"Yet DMan denied it," Steve said.

"Yes, and the question is why?" I looked over at Gabe, but he was staring out the window. I couldn't imagine what was going through his head. If I'd spent years with a band and then they lied about something, I'd be upset too.

"We should get a copy of the songs Gabe wrote in case the band killed Gabe for them," Steve said.

"Whoa. Since when do you make up theories? That's what Glinda and I do."

He chuckled. "You are right. I got carried away. All this talk of ghosts and vampires has me off my game."

"I understand." I turned to Gabe. "Where are the songs you just wrote?"

"At home on my computer and on some sheet music I scribbled on."

"We should get them." I told Steve my plan. "If The Rebels killed Gabe for the music, we'll find out soon enough. They have a concert this weekend in Tampa."

"Interesting. But sure. Get a copy of the music. It could prove useful."

When we arrived back at the sheriff's office, I slipped out of his vehicle. "I'm going to head back to Nicky. Between all of us, we should be able to find Gabe's music for you."

"Thanks. You know I'd do it myself, but I can't see or hear Gabe, and I'd need him to give me his computer password and stuff."

I nodded. Gabe could tell him the password right now, but Steve still wouldn't know where to look. We needed Gabe for that.

I crossed the street and went upstairs to the office. Nicky was sitting on the floor with Iggy playing cards. Really? Iggy couldn't easily turn over a card, let alone hold them.

"Hey."

They both looked up.

"I beat Nicky in War."

I used to play War all the time. "How did you do that?"

"Nicky turns the cards over for me."

"Ahh. Well, if you both aren't too tired, we have a job to do."

Nicky jumped up. "Can we scour Gabe's home and office for some goodies now?"

"Yes." I told them about our discussion with DMan and the band. "Something is off, though. Very off."

"They're lying. Just say it," Gabe said.

It was nice that I was with people—and a familiar—who could hear and see Gabe. "I honestly don't know that. Unless my internal radar is way off, I actually believed DMan."

Gabe paced. "I don't, but if your sheriff has my phone, he should see the call I made to DMan a few days ago lasted several minutes."

"What does that prove?"

"A song lasts about three minutes. We talked for at least ten."

That still didn't prove anything. "Let's see what we find at your house and go from there. If we assume one theory is better than another, we might miss something."

He kind of shrugged. "If I'm to believe Bella, then you are good at this murder stuff."

I practically blushed. And here, I didn't think Bella thought all that highly of me. "I'll drive."

"Wait," he said.

"What?"

"I live in a gated community, and you'll need permission to enter. Unfortunately, I can't give it."

That could be a problem. "Let me call Steve. Maybe he can call over there. What's the name of the place?"

Gabe gave me the information, and then I called Steve and explained that we wanted to check out Gabe's place for his music. "Can you make sure we can get past the gate?"

"It's not in my jurisdiction, but I can contact the sheriff there. I'm sure he can give the guardhouse a call."

"Thanks." I disconnected. "We're all set. Ready?"

I didn't even ask Iggy if he wanted to go. I knew the answer. I picked him up and Nicky followed us out.

"Where are Bella and Lorenzo?" Iggy asked.

"They're spying on the band."

"How will they find us?" Iggy seemed worried.

"Worst case, we'll meet back here."

I drove and followed Gabe's instructions to his housing complex. True to his word, Steve had managed to get us an invitation inside. Clearly, it helped to know the right people.

Once we parked in Gabe's driveway, he told us where he kept his spare key. Nicky located it and let us in.

As soon as we stepped inside, we all froze.

"What the—" Gabe was clearly upset, and I couldn't blame him. He sped over to the living room bookcase where many of the books were on the floor.

"Someone was looking for something. Maybe you should look in your office too." I assumed he had one.

Nicky followed him in while Iggy and I checked out the rest of the house. The place was a little musty, but that was to be expected since he hadn't been there to air it out.

I set Iggy down while I looked in the kitchen. Thankfully,

everything looked intact. And neat. Very neat, which I found odd for a bachelor, though Gavin was almost as neat.

Iggy waddled in. "Where's the dog?"

"What dog?"

"There's dog hair on the floor."

That would be terrible if an owner died and the pet couldn't get out. I briefly looked at the doors leading to the back, but I didn't notice any doggie doors.

"It could be human hair," I said.

"No. It's short and thick. Definitely animal."

Iggy was an expert now? "Let's ask Gabe."

I picked up Iggy and found Gabe and Nicky in the office where she was at the desk studying the laptop. "Give me a sec. I think I found them," Nicky said.

"You found the songs?" I asked.

"I hope so."

Gabe moved closer to Nicky. "They're under Maria. That's my adoptive mom's name. I figured no one would think to look there."

Nicky clicked a few keys as Iggy and I moved behind her. "Open the folder to see if his music is there."

I didn't know why it wouldn't be, unless some nefarious person erased the contents.

She clicked on the folder and stilled.

chapter
ten

"WAIT A MINUTE. WHERE ARE THE SONGS?"
Gabe asked.

"The folder is empty. Are you sure this is where you saved them?" she asked.

"Yes. I'm positive. Look in the trash folder."

Nicky clicked on the trashcan icon, but it was completely empty. "Someone dumped the trash."

"See if they moved the songs." Though I didn't know why they would have.

"I'll look." After a long search on the rest of the computer, the songs were nowhere to be found, which was unfortunate.

"I'm sorry, Gabe. Nicky, how about taking a screen shot to show Steve? What he can do with it, I don't know, but it seems to point a finger at a band member."

"I bet if Jaxson were here, he'd be able to find them. Just because you delete something, it doesn't mean it's really gone."

"True. We'll let the sheriff in this town deal with it," I said.

"Gabe, you said you liked to hand write the songs. Do you have any of that music?" I asked.

He spun around and grinned. "You, Rihanna Samuels, are a genius."

I had no idea why he thought so. Even if he found a handwritten version on his songs, he wouldn't be playing them—at least not in this realm. "Why is that?"

"If we can find them, we can prove that someone stole *my* songs. Find that person, and we might learn who killed me."

"That's a thought, but if magic is involved, it's really hard to bring that person to justice."

"That's okay. At least I'd know who did it."

"Ask Gabe about his dog. I'm worried," Iggy said.

Gabe floated over to Iggy. "A dog? I don't have a dog."

"Iggy found dog hair on the floor."

Gabe shook his head. "I'm allergic to cats and dogs. Even if I hadn't been, I work too many long hours to care for a pet. It wouldn't have been fair to the animal."

"I get it. I'm glad Iggy can come and go as he pleases, though Glinda takes Iggy most places."

"That's what she likes you to believe."

Now he was being childish.

"I don't think I tracked in any dog hair—when I was alive, that is. Besides, Carla comes once a week to clean." His eyes widened. "Dang it. I need to call her and tell her I no longer need her services."

I waited for him to realize the flaw in his thinking. When he didn't say anything, I decided to offer. "Would you like me to call her?"

He huffed. "That would be great. I forgot that I can't call anymore."

"I'm afraid not."

He told me her number that I entered into my phone. "Carla has worked for you for a long time I take it?" He sounded fond of her.

"Eleven years."

"Wow! I'll be sure to call her tonight."

"Thanks."

I looked around. "Where did you keep your handwritten songs?" I asked.

"In the living room." His eyes widened. "Maybe that's why the place was a mess."

That wasn't good. "Who knew you kept your songs there?"

"Everyone in the band."

"You haven't been in the band for ten years," I said.

"I know, but I've lived in this house that long. They all used to come over here."

"Even Sev?" Nicky asked. "I thought he was new."

"Excellent point. All but Sev."

That might put him at the bottom of the guilty list.

"What about Carla?" Nicky asked. "Could she have done this?"

"No way. She might have worked for me for a long time. Besides, I paid her very well."

"We should at least temporarily cross Carla off the suspect list." I had to decide where to begin sorting through this mess. "Did you leave your songs in a drawer, in a book, under the sofa cushion, or someplace else—like a false floorboard?"

"I wasn't that devious. I would fold them up and put them in a book."

The pieces were starting to fall into place. "Let's see if they missed any songs."

Nicky hadn't moved. "Shouldn't we call Steve? This is a robbery, you know."

Darn. She was right. Kind of. "This isn't Steve's jurisdiction, and who knows what the sheriff here would do. Let's look around first. When we get back to town, we'll tell Steve, and he can call the sheriff."

Nicky smiled. "I like the way you think, but don't forget

to remind him to have a technical person check out the computer for the deleted files."

"I will."

We spent about half an hour opening every book on the shelves. Most of the books he remembered stashing the songs in were already on the floor.

"I found one," Nicky shouted.

"Great!" I moved next to her. I read the title. "Dreaming of You."

"That's one of the new ones."

I took a picture of it and sent it to Steve. "Maybe I should keep this as evidence. What's to stop this person from coming back here?"

"Good point. If they saw *Dreaming of You* on my computer, they might wonder where it is."

"You should give it to Hugo," Iggy suggested. "That's better than putting it in a safe."

I smiled. "You might be right, but let's see what Steve wants to do first."

"I hope he won't turn it over to this other sheriff," Nicky said.

"I bet not. Gabe died in our jurisdiction, but I can't say for sure who has the right to Gabe's stuff. I say we play dumb."

Nicky laughed. "You go, girl."

Gabe looked around. "I can't believe I'm dead, and that this is really happening. It's so depressing."

Death usually was, but I wasn't sure what prompted this emotion? Seeing the house a mess, or realizing that someone would have to pick up the pieces of his life. "Do you have a relative who can sell the house for you?"

He shook his head. "There's no one. Sad, huh?"

"Yes. I should have thought of this before, but do you have a will? Money is a good motivator for murder."

"I do, but I made it out a long time ago. Since my parents

are deceased, I donated my net worth to the band—to be divided among the three members that were with me at the time."

I whistled. "Do they know this?"

"They do."

This stasis idea might be all wrong. "If you had the chance to redo the will, who would you donate the money to?"

He shrugged. "It's a moot point now, but I wouldn't give it to the band, assuming they are responsible for my death."

"We don't know for sure anyone from The Rebels killed you, though. If we believe in the vampire theory, one of them might have wanted to keep you alive for a few days before resurrecting you. I can't imagine their reasoning, however."

"I agree. How would having me out of the picture for a few days change anything? I still would have wanted to get out of the financial planning business. The job was way too stressful."

"If Bella and Lorenzo were here, they might have a suggestion." Iggy tapped my leg to get my attention. "Yes?" I asked as I picked him up.

"Maybe the hair on the floor belongs to the killer's pet."

I looked over at Nicky hoping she'd have a comeback.

"Iggy, I don't think a thief would have a pet with him if his intention was to rob the place," she said.

"Maybe it was a watch dog." He lifted his head.

Okay, that had potential. "Tell you what. How about we gather some of the hair? Maybe Elissa or Steve can figure out what kind of pet it is."

If he could have smiled, he would have. "Good thinking."

I unfolded the sheet of music. "Show me where this hair is."

"Put me down, and I will."

Boy, was he ever demanding today, but I was happy to let

him play detective. The floor was hardwood, which would make it easier to pick up this dog hair.

"There." Iggy placed his claw close to it.

I scooped it up. It was short and brownish red in color. Only because I wanted to appease him did I go along with this new theory of his. "Was there only one hair?"

"No. There were a few." With his snout to the ground, he found a few more.

I picked up the evidence and placed the hairs in the music paper. They certainly seemed to be animal hair. "That should be enough. How about we show this to Steve?"

"I thought we were going to check out Gabe's office for the addresses of the three disgruntled clients," Nicky said.

"We can do that. It's on the way," Gabe said.

"Then sure." I snapped my fingers. "If someone robbed your house, wouldn't they have to check in with the guardhouse?"

"Yes, unless they were on the list of people I allowed in. I filled it out when I first moved in here, and never thought to update it."

"Don't tell me everyone in the band is on the list."

"Yup," he said.

Maybe Gabe was secretly hoping his band would visit, though the security service should have insisted he update it. "You're no help." I turned to Nicky. "Remind me to ask Steve to ask the local sheriff if he can get the list of people who came to Gabe's house recently."

She saluted me.

When we stepped outside, I was about to put the spare key back in its hiding place, but then thought better of it. "I'll give the key to Steve, if that's okay with you, Gabe. You never know when or if this person decides to return. He might realize that he's missing one of your songs."

"Smart."

I pocketed the key, and we headed to the car. Once we were underway, Gabe gave me instructions to his office, which might actually be in Steve's jurisdiction.

It was located in an ordinary strip mall. To be honest, I would have expected him to be in a more upscale place considering his home was quite nice, and his job catered to a more affluent type of person, or so I assumed.

We parked, and I got out.

"My office is unit L."

He'd said his office door had a keypad, which seemed safer than a key. When we stood in front of the door, I looked up at Gabe. "I'll need the code."

"Oh, yeah."

A few offices away a door opened and an older lady stepped out. She looked up and waddled toward us. Uh-oh.

"Gabe isn't here," she announced, proud of her knowledge. Thankfully, this woman had an open mind. She just wanted to be helpful.

"That's the busy body, Agnes Lentman. She runs the water purification shop. Tell her I gave you the code."

I smiled and held out my hand. "You must be Agnes. I'm Rihanna."

That seemed to take the steam out of her. "Have we met?"

"Gabe told me about you."

"Like I said, Gabe isn't here. I haven't seen him in days."

She must not read the news or listen to gossip. "I know. Gabe passed away a few days ago. He said if anything happened to him that I needed to secure some of his things."

Agnes gasped. "He's dead?" She took a few steps back and looked as if she was going to fall.

Quick thinking Nicky clasped Agnes' arm to steady her. "Maybe you should sit down."

"I'll be okay. Just give me a second. How did he die?"

As was often the case, I didn't need to be a mind reader to see that she was truly upset. "We don't know."

She pressed her lips together. "Gabe was such a nice young man."

"Really? She usually found something to complain about me," he said.

"He was," I answered. "I need to gather some records and mail them to a friend for safekeeping." I hope she bought that lie.

She nodded to the door. "He gave you the code?"

"Yes." I looked up at him.

"It's 5-6-0-1-4-2," Gabe said.

I punched in the numbers, hoping I remembered them correctly. When the door clicked open, I sighed and turned to Agnes. "You should rest a bit. I can see Gabe's death came as a shock."

"It did." She turned around and slowly walked back to her store.

Nicky and I stepped inside. "Phew, that was close."

"We should have asked if she saw anyone sneaking around," Nicky said.

"Why would they if they found Gabe's music already?"

"I don't know."

"Ladies, we came for the addresses of my clients, remember?"

"Right." I followed him to his desk. Thankfully, his office looked undisturbed. "What's going to happen to your clients now that you're...you know?"

"Dead?" I nodded. "Maybe your sheriff can call them or something. They'll have to find someone else to handle their investments."

"Whoever it is will need access to their records."

"True. You should make a note of the keypad combination so you or the sheriff can get in if need be," he said.

That was very trusting of him. "Sure." I pulled out my phone and asked him to repeat the combination so I could enter it in my notes. "Thanks," I said to him after he did.

Gabe floated over to his desk. "I'm kind of old-fashioned in that I like to keep paper records of some things. Nicky, if you open the top desk drawer, you'll find a key that unlocks my file cabinet."

She pulled open the drawer, pawned through a few things, and lifted a key. "This it?"

"Yes. It's the second file drawer from the top. My clients are listed alphabetically. You should take Mona Leanders', Arnie Driscoll's, and Pamela Vetters' files. If you find out the band is innocent of my death, then I'd look into these three."

The front office door opened and a tall man, about Gabe's age, strode in. "What's going on?"

He did not sound happy. I could almost hear Iggy lecturing me on why hadn't I asked Hugo to accompany me.

chapter
eleven

I COULDN'T HELP but look over at Gabe for some help.

"That's Elliot Warfel. He is also a financial advisor. I bet he came to see if he could take my files so he could pinch my clients."

The newcomer laughed but quickly sobered. Squinting, he walked closer, his gaze on Gabe and not on us.

"Gabe?" he asked.

Holy moly? He could see him? Well, I guess so since he called out his name.

Gabe moved closer to his acquaintance. "You can see me?"

"Barely. You're a...ghost? I mean I heard you'd died, but I never believed ghosts existed."

"Yeah. That's why I'm here with my friends. I want to see if we can figure out who killed me."

Elliot stabbed a hand through his hair. "I can't believe it. How did it happen?"

Hadn't Gabe just said that Nicky and I were there to help him figure out the answer to that question? I needed to say something. "I take it you're a warlock?"

Elliot faced me. "Yeah, but I don't practice or anything. I

mean, my mom is a witch, but she didn't embrace her talents. I take it you two girls are witches too?"

I wasn't sure how many other options there were. Bella came from a family of voodoo priestesses, and I'd heard of sorcerers and other magical beings, but I'd never met any.

"Yes," Nicky said. "We were the ones who found Gabe. We volunteered to help him learn who killed him."

"Where did you die, Gabe?" Elliot asked.

I wish I could crawl into his mind and figure out what he was thinking, but he wasn't allowing me to do that. People of magic seemed better able to block me than ordinary people.

Gabe gave Elliot a brief outline of the events that led up to his death.

"We are pretty convinced that a person of magic either killed Gabe or put him into a state of stasis." I explained what that meant.

If it hadn't been for our photo project, I bet no one would have entered that place for months if not longer. Of course, some teenagers might still be using the house as a place to party.

"I know nothing about that kind of magic." He held up a hand. "On a different note, Mona Leanders came to see me two days ago," Elliot said.

The hairs on my arms stood up.

"I'm not surprised," Gabe said. "I still feel terrible that my sources didn't pan out about one of my stock picks. It was Cloud 9 that she invested heavily in."

Elliot laughed. "Pan out? Is that what you call a fifty percent dump?"

"There was nothing I could have done. Once the FDA approval didn't come through, the stock tanked."

Elliot stepped closer to Gabe. "Did you at least warn her this could happen? She'd just lost her husband, you know."

Even though I'd not met any of Gabe's clients, I felt bad for Gabe and them.

"Of course I did, but Mona said she was willing to take the risk. Hey, I only make the suggestions. I leave the final decision up to the client."

"She told me that," Elliot admitted. "However, you shouldn't have mentioned such a risky stock in the first place."

"In hindsight, I'd say you are right."

"Was Mona mad enough to want to kill Gabe?" I asked.

Elliot spun to face me. "Kill Gabe? Heck no. In fact, she was upset that Gabe was dead. You should know that Mona is a tiny, sweet woman who wouldn't hurt a fly."

So was Gertrude Poole, our ninety-year-old Witch's Cove resident psychic, but I bet she could do some damage if she set her mind to it. "You wouldn't happen to know if she is a witch by any chance."

His head tilt said it all. "I am a professional financial advisor. It's not the standard question I ask my clients. And speaking of my clients, did you know that Mona used to be mine before Gabe stole her from me?"

Whoa. This was becoming juicier by the minute.

Gabe floated closer to Elliot. "Did you know that Mona threatened to have my license revoked?"

Elliot shook his head. "No. She never mentioned it."

Iggy crawled out from under the desk. I was sure he was looking for more dog hair, convinced Gabe was hiding something.

"Can you hear me?" Iggy asked.

Elliot didn't respond. Since not all witches could see all ghosts, I'd concluded that not all people of magic could communicate with familiars. I lifted Iggy and placed him on the desk.

As expected, Elliot's eyes widened. "Gabe, is that your pet or something?"

I answered. "No. Iggy is mine. Well, I'm pet sitting for my cousin."

Iggy looked over at me. "You will pay for that slight. Pet sitting indeed."

I worked hard not to smile. I returned my attention to the newcomer. "Mr. Warfel, were you the financial advisor for any of Gabe's other clients?"

"A few. This man can be a charmer. Gabe is excellent at convincing people that he can provide them with a higher return for their money."

"That's because I usually could," Gabe shot back.

"Until you didn't. But I get it. The stock market hasn't been kind this past year, what with cryptos coming onto the market, inflation, and other restrictions. I can't say my stock picks grew by leaps and bounds either, but at least they didn't bankrupt people."

I spun to face Gabe. "Be honest. Did you ever promise some of your clients things you couldn't deliver on?"

"No! I mean, maybe, but only a little. Look, no one can predict with any certainty what the market will do. I just give my best guess. Trust me, I warned them that nothing in the market is a sure thing."

"What about Arnie Driscoll? You said he might have had something to do with your death."

Elliot crossed his arms. "I warned Arnie not to jump ship and go with Gabe, but did he listen? No."

I had the sense these two had been competing for clients for a long time. It seemed as if Elliot was quite conservative, while Gabe was a more aggressive investor.

When Gabe explained that Arnie had borrowed the money from his brother, Elliot whistled. "Do you think Arnie could have killed you?" Elliot asked.

"I don't know."

"Elliot," I said. "Why did you come here today if you were

aware that Gabe was dead?" Several other questions then bombarded me. "And how did you expect to get in?"

Gabe smiled. "Yeah. Answer that."

The newcomer faced me. "I'll start with how I expected to get in. Gabe tells too many people his keypad combination."

"I never told you."

"No, but I was standing next to you one time when you pressed the buttons. You really should be more careful."

Too late now.

Gabe waved a watery hand. "Elliot is right. I never thought I had anything really important in here, which is why I wasn't all that careful."

"The clients' records are confidential." There was no use arguing with a dead man. I turned to Elliot. "So why come?"

"To be honest, with Gabe dead, I thought I'd jot down his clients' names and contact information so I could call them."

"I'm glad you came then. You're a good financial advisor. If I had been as conservative as you this whole time, maybe my clients wouldn't have lost money."

I hadn't expected that confession. "Before we hand over any files or names to Elliot, we need to let the sheriff have first dibs." I turned to this other financial advisor. "As we mentioned, there is a chance that one of Gabe's clients killed him."

Elliot held up his hands. "Then by all means, keep their files. When all the loose ends are tied up, let me know." He pulled a wallet out of his pocket and fished out a business card. "Here. Contact me. I know a few of his clients, so I might be able to help if you need any background information on them."

That might be helpful. She gave him her number in case he thought of something. "Thanks."

"Have you ever done a spell?" Nicky asked out of the blue.

"Me?" He shrugged. "I tried a few of them about twenty

years ago but failed at all of them. It wasn't something I wanted to be good at. That's why I had no idea I could see ghosts—until I saw Gabe, that is. Why Gabe? Who knows? It could be because I've known him since we were six."

That was interesting. "I've heard that if people are close, they can sometimes see the deceased." Bella's dad had been able to connect somewhat with her because of how close they were. That might be why I couldn't see my father—assuming he'd appeared. But Nicky and her grandmother were super tight, and yet she hasn't seen her grandmother's ghost, so my theory might be way off.

Elliot waved a hand. "I should be going. Call me if you need me."

"I will." The fact he was a warlock implied he might have been the one to kill Gabe, but my gut said no. However, I didn't have a long enough track record with solving murders to really know.

I turned to Nicky and Gabe. "Ready to give these files—or at least the three most important files—to Steve?"

"Sure," Nicky said.

When Gabe didn't answer, I wondered if he wanted us to look at something. "Gabe? Is there anything else?"

He looked around, his lips pressed together. "No, it's just that while this office wasn't much, it had been my life for the last ten years. I'm going to miss it."

That was sad. "I guess you could always visit."

"Nah. The landlord will rent it to someone else, taking my memories with him."

"Then don't come back. Keep all of your memories in your heart."

I picked up Iggy. "That was so sappy," he murmured.

I looked down at him. "Is that so? If Glinda and Jaxson moved away from Witch's Cove to some place really cool, wouldn't you miss our office and your apartment?"

He looked up at me. "Is that a trick question?"

"No. Would you miss it?"

"I guess, but I'd miss the people more."

"See? I bet that was what Gabe meant too."

Gabe moved over to Iggy and floated down to his eye level. "Rihanna is right. I do miss the people most of all."

"Whatever," Iggy said.

He'd been hanging around Bella too much. "Let's drop off these files at Steve's office—assuming he is still at work—and tell him about the break-in at Gabe's home. Then I will see what Bella and Lorenzo have to say."

When no one added anything, we left. I let Nicky hold the important files. I located a piece of paper in my glove compartment. "Nicky, even though I have the keypad number in my phone, it will be easier if you jot down the combination for Steve."

"I can do that."

Gabe gave her the information again, and she scribbled it down. Thankfully, it didn't take us long to return to Witch's Cove. I parked at our office, more or less across the street from the sheriff's office.

"Iggy, do you want to come with us to see Steve or go upstairs?"

"Are you kidding me? Did you forget who found those dog hairs?"

I didn't know why he was so fixated on them, but I didn't want to assume they weren't important. "Fine. Come with us."

Nicky and I crossed the street and entered the sheriff's department. Jennifer Larson was manning the front desk since Pearl's shift had ended. "We have some information for Steve regarding the Gabe Rebel murder."

"Sure. Go on back."

When we entered his office, Steve glanced at Iggy. "Detective Iggy. Did you figure out who killed Gabe yet?"

"Why do people always ask me that? I'm just a lizard."

I had to laugh at that one. "I'll remind you of that the next time you tell us you are the only smart one around."

Iggy didn't respond as Nicky and I sat down. "We have a lot of news," I stated.

"Someone broke into Gabe's house and stole his music," Nicky blurted.

"What? Why didn't you call me?"

I shouldn't have been surprised he'd react that way. "It's not your jurisdiction."

The sheriff huffed. "Did you contact the sheriff there then?"

"No. I figured you could do that." I placed the key to Gabe's house on Steve's desk. "In case you want to take a look."

He put the key in his drawer. "Thanks. Tell me everything."

Between the four of us, we gave a detailed description of what we found and where, including the fact the songs appeared to have been deleted.

"Don't forget the dog hair," Iggy said.

"Dog hair?" Steve asked.

I placed the folded sheet music on Steve's desk. "Iggy found this hair on the floor. Gabe has no pets, so we can't explain it."

"I bet it belongs to the killer's pet," Iggy said.

Steve was clearly trying to keep a straight face. "I'll send the evidence over to Elissa. She might have the ability to tell us what kind of animal it belongs to."

"Thanks," I said. "We figured that whoever broke into Gabe's house would have had to have gone through security. I doubt the guard will give us a list of visitors, but maybe you or the local sheriff could find out."

Steve pulled out his yellow notepad and jotted down a few notes. "I'll definitely get that list. Anything else?"

Nicky put a pile of folders on his desk. "These are the three clients of Gabe's that he thinks might have wanted to harm him."

"I see. I'll look into them."

"Tell him about Elliot," Gabe tossed in.

"Oh, yes. While we were at Gabe's office, someone came in. That someone is a warlock."

Steve whistled. "You know the drill. Start from the beginning."

chapter
twelve

BETWEEN ALL OF US, I was confident we had detailed the entire conversation we had with Elliot.

"What's your gut reaction to this Elliot Warfel man?" Steve asked.

I looked up at Gabe. "What's your take on your friend—if you can call him that."

"He's sneaky and smart, but I don't see him as a killer. I heard his business wasn't doing as well as it had been, but then again, neither was mine. Like I told you, I planned to get out of the financial business."

"Would you recommend Elliot to your clients now that you're no longer available?" I asked more for Steve's sake.

Gabe seemed to think about it. "I'd have to say I would."

That spoke volumes. I relayed to Steve what Gabe thought about Elliot.

He took notes. "What about you three? Get any vibes off the guy?"

I thought it was sweet that he included Iggy in the discussion. "I only met him for a few minutes. If he hadn't been able to see Gabe, I never would have known he was a warlock." I lifted a hand. "But that doesn't mean I think he put the spell on Gabe."

Steve's brows pinched. "Good to know, but you said he can see ghosts?"

"He could see Gabe. Elliot said it was his first experience with a ghost."

"That must have been scary for him. Good thing you three —or four—were there to confirm he wasn't hallucinating."

I looked over at Nicky and nodded. She was chomping at the bit to give her take. "Go ahead."

"Elliot was fidgeting a lot, but I didn't sense his heart rate was spiking. He might not have *seen* ghosts before, but he might have *felt* their presence in the past."

Steve took more notes. "I'll check out these clients, as well as this Elliot guy."

"Just to keep you up to speed, both Bella and Lorenzo spent the day with the band to see what gossip they could gather. We're headed back now to find out what they have learned."

"If it is relevant, call me." He pulled out his business card and jotted down his cell. "For emergencies. This way you won't have to go through Pearl or Jennifer."

"I appreciate that."

The four of us headed out. No surprise, Gabe shot over to the office in a flash. I guess he wanted to get the scoop from Bella and Lorenzo, assuming they'd returned, before we did.

As I crossed the street, my stomach grumbled. "We haven't eaten since breakfast. How about I call in for pizza delivery?"

Nicky grinned. "That would be perfect."

To my delight, both Bella and Lorenzo were in the office when we arrived.

"About time you got here." Bella sounded a little upset but also a bit excited.

"Let me call in our dinner order, and then we will

exchange information." Once I asked Nicky what she wanted, I made the call. "Our meal will be here in twenty-five minutes."

"Great."

Iggy crawled toward Lorenzo. "You learn anything?"

Iggy was impatient, just like Glinda.

"Not as much as we'd have liked. No one was bragging about killing Gabe or putting him in any kind of stasis," Lorenzo said.

"Did anyone seem upset that I died?"

I wanted to hug the man for all the emotional pain he was going through, but of course that was impossible.

"They seemed to wish you were there to help them with a new song."

New song? "You don't happen to remember the name of the song, do you?" I asked.

"No, but it had a sad, yet relatable melody," Lorenzo said.

I looked over at Bella. She'd be more aware of the titles than Lorenzo. "Do you know?"

"Hmm. Not exactly, but it talked about some guy wishing he was with some woman."

"*Meet Me Tomorrow*?" Gabe asked.

"Yes! That was it." Bella seemed excited that she remembered.

I waited for Gabe to tell me the meaning of that. "Gabe?"

"That was the song I sang to DMan over the phone."

"That means someone did steal your song." And someone lied about it.

"Yes, only I can't prove it since we didn't find the hand-written song in my books on my bookshelves or on my computer."

Bella floated over to him. "Maybe I have the name wrong. Can you sing it for us?"

"Without a guitar, I might not sound great."

Like that mattered? "Give it a try."

Gabe cleared his throat and did a quick scale practice. "Okay. Here goes." He closed his eyes and started singing.

Aunt Fern was right. His voice was divine. I became so carried away that I forgot to listen to all of the words. When he finished, Nicky clapped and Bella tried to.

"That was it!" Bella said.

I wasn't sure if it was a good thing that Gabe's former band members had stolen from him—and had possibly killed him—but it was what it was.

"I can't believe it," he said. "We need to find out who is responsible."

I looked over at Bella and Lorenzo. "Did any one of the band members mention how they received this song? Did one of them claim Gabe gave it to them?"

Bella and Lorenzo shook their heads. "It was as if they'd had it for a while."

"That's not possible," Gabe said. "I wrote it less than two weeks ago."

"Wait a second," Bella said. "I think Sev said he wrote it."

"Sev has written songs before," Gabe said, "but they've never been any good."

"Compared to your talent, maybe that's true," I said. "Do you think DMan, Rod, and Steely believed the song was his?"

Gabe looked over at Lorenzo and Bella, but I don't know how he'd think they'd know. He faced me. "Maybe. They aren't going to consider that I wrote the song, especially since it has a different vibe from what I used to write. I want to know why DMan didn't speak up? He knew I was writing again."

That was the big question.

Iggy crawled on top of the coffee table. "You know what this reminds me of?" he asked.

This should be good. "No, what?"

"Remember when Hugo's host walked out of the store, and when Andorra came back she remembered nothing? The same thing happened to Elissa. Her memory was erased too."

Whoa. That was a thought. "It would take a witch or warlock to do that."

"I don't know anyone who has magic—other than Elliot. Though his announcement was news to me," Gabe said. "It might explain why DMan claimed he hadn't heard my song. I know I sang it to him, but then the person who killed me must have erased his memory so DMan wouldn't know Sev hadn't written the song."

That was a bit convoluted, but I think I understood it. "Could Sev be a warlock?" I asked, then looked over at Bella and Lorenzo. "He'd have the most to gain by erasing DMan's memory."

"How could I tell if he didn't do a spell or anything when we were there?" Bella asked.

"You couldn't." Darn. I wish we could tell who had powers and who didn't. It was what frustrated Glinda when she was trying to solve a crime.

"You know what the most irritating thing is?" Gabe said.

There were a lot of things, I would imagine. "What?"

"I can't prove that I wrote the song."

"You could sing it for Steve," Bella said.

"Bella, Steve can't hear Gabe."

"Oh, yeah. Why do I keep forgetting we're dead? When we're working on a case, I almost feel alive."

I smiled. "You seem alive to me too."

"I've got it," Gabe said. "I have several songs on my phone. Can you ask your sheriff to check?"

"That's awesome. I'll call him now." Using his private number, I called him.

"Did you find something?" he asked as a way of saying hello.

"I did." I explained what Bella and Lorenzo heard. "Gabe says he thinks that song might still be on his phone. Can you check?"

"I am on my way home, but I for sure will look tomorrow."

While I was a little disappointed, time wasn't critical. "Thanks."

As soon as I disconnected, Bella floated up to me. "What did he say?"

I explained that he'd look tomorrow. "You all did a great job today. Thank you."

"We know we can't do much tonight, and soon you'll need to go to bed, but we don't," Bella said. "The three of us will have an all-night brainstorming session while you snooze the night away."

"I'm sure my mind will be working too." I appreciated that both Bella and Lorenzo were so willing to help solve this case for someone they'd just met.

"Not so fast, Bella," Lorenzo said. "Rihanna, Nicky, Iggy, and Gabe never told us what they all learned."

I gave them a quick recap, but they'd already heard that Gabe had some songs stolen and that Elliot, another financial advisor, was a warlock. I just filled in the gaps.

"I'm even more confused than before," Lorenzo said.

"About something in particular?" I asked.

"I'm not sure. This whole stasis thing doesn't seem to fit."

"Which part? The fact that Gabe might not be a vampire or the fact the killer wasn't trying to put him into stasis with the plan to bring him back to life?"

"Yes."

"Yes to which part?" Ghosts could be so unclear.

Lorenzo crossed his wispy arms. "To the second part. I still believe Gabe is a vampire, not that it makes much of a difference now, but I can't decide if this person meant to kill Gabe or not."

"When we find out who harmed him, we'll ask." Not that anyone would confess.

"Okay."

I loved how innocent Lorenzo was. "By any chance did the band mention if they were planning to perform Gabe's song in Tampa this weekend?" I asked.

Bella nodded. "I can't say for sure, but they all seemed excited about the upcoming show."

I looked over at Nicky. "Do you have any interest in a road trip to Tampa—assuming we can get tickets?"

"Are you kidding? I'd love to go."

Someone knocked on the door. "That must be the pizza guy."

I grabbed my purse and opened the door. Once I paid the delivery boy, I carried in the food, and my stomach grumbled at the delicious smell.

"I have an idea," Lorenzo said to his two cohorts.

I set the food on the coffee table, and Nicky helped me open up the box.

"What's that?" Bella asked.

"What if for a few hours, we show Gabe what New Orleans is like. It might cheer him up."

I glanced over at Gabe, hoping he'd appreciate the gesture.

"I'm game," the recently departed stated.

"As long as this isn't a ploy to get more help in looking for that stupid coffin of yours, I think it's a brilliant idea," Bella added.

"My dear, you offend me. I was planning on showing Gabe my family's casinos."

"Fine. Let's go." Bella said. "We'll be back tomorrow morning."

I loved that she was willing to give me some space. Bella hadn't learned that concept when she first became a ghost.

With that they disappeared.

I swallowed a smile. "Let me get some plates."

Iggy followed me. "I need to make sure you give me lettuce. You aren't the best at remembering things."

I had forgotten a few times, mostly because I wasn't used to having to watch the little bugger twenty-four seven. "Don't worry. I won't let you starve."

Once I fixed a plate for Iggy, I returned with extra napkins and some plates should we need them.

"I'm glad you volunteered to call Carla," Nicky said. "Having to tell someone they don't have a job anymore will be tough."

"I know. If she worked for Gabe for so many years, she probably knew him pretty well."

"Do you think she'll have any idea who killed him?"

I huffed out a laugh. "Why would she?"

"Maids overhear a lot of things, like phone conversations."

"True. After we finish eating, I'll call. Maybe she'll shed some light on something important."

During the rest of the meal, we discussed a few things I might ask Carla. Once my nerves settled, I dialed her number.

"Hello?"

"Is this Carla?"

"Yes."

"I'm not sure if you've heard or not, but Gabe Rebel passed away recently."

Something shattered on the floor. "Oh, no."

I wasn't sure if she was responding to the broken item, or if she was truly upset over his death. "I'm very sorry."

"How did he die?"

"We don't know." I explained that Nicky and I were doing a photo shoot when we found him.

"That is terrible. He was such a nice man."

"I didn't know him. However, the sheriff said someone had ransacked his house and stolen some of his music. I trust when you last left, his place was clean."

"For sure. I clean every Saturday."

That didn't provide me with any better time of death. "Did Gabe have any friends over who had a dog? We found a bunch of hairs on the living room floor."

"No. Mr. Gabe is allergic to cats and dogs. Everyone knows that, which is why I wash the floors every time I'm there."

That kind of pointed the finger at the killer having a dog. But who would have an animal with them when stealing music? Was it to make the person appear friendlier should they be stopped by a neighbor?

"Did Gabe tell a lot of people about his songs?" I asked.

"No. He wanted to surprise his old band."

"So no one from his band came over in the last few weeks?" I asked.

"All I know is that no one was at his house when I was there."

That made sense. "Did Gabe mention if anyone was angry with him?"

Carla said nothing for a moment. "I heard a heated conversation about a week ago."

"Did you know what it was about?"

"His work."

So not about his music. "I see. A sheriff might be calling you for more information," I said.

"Why me? I just worked for Mr. Gabe. That's all."

"Oh, I know. You didn't do anything wrong. The sheriff thinks you might have overheard or seen things you aren't even aware of. That's all." While part of what I said was true, some of it was a lie.

"Okay." She sniffled.

"I just wanted to call and let you know. Again, I'm sorry for your loss."

"Thanks."

I hung up before she asked me who I was, and why was I calling her instead of someone from the sheriff's department. I faced Nicky. "She didn't say much. I sensed she didn't know much either."

"That stinks."

"We'll find some clues. At least Glinda always does."

chapter
thirteen

THE NEXT MORNING, Bella woke me. "Rihanna, get up. We have work to do."

Ugh. I leaned over and glanced at my phone. It was after eight, which was late for me. I guess I was more tired than I thought. "Give me a few minutes to dress. I also need to call Steve."

"Okay."

Only she didn't leave, which implied she might have more to tell me. "Did you and the boys have fun last night?"

"Yes. It was awesome. Lorenzo's family's casino is incredible. People were gambling, drinking, and partying. There were lights, music, and so much joy. I loved it."

"And Gabe? What did he think?"

"There was a band that he really liked. I think he had a good time."

"Great. Did the three of you think of anything earth-shattering about who might have harmed Gabe while you were having a good time?"

"Not really."

So much for the ghosts helping to brainstorm. "By the

way, I contacted Carla, Gabe's maid, last night and told her about his death."

"I bet she was sad." I nodded. "Did she know anything?"

"No, other than Gabe never let a dog in the house, and the last time she was there, the place was clean."

"That wasn't very helpful."

"It might be. Give me a minute to see if Steve found any songs on Gabe's phone."

"Okay."

I crawled out of bed and went over to my chest of drawers. "How about giving me some privacy?"

"Sheesh. Be that way." Bella huffed and then left.

I didn't know why I asked her to leave, but I was used to dressing by myself. I located my phone and called the sheriff.

"Rihanna, I was just about to call you to say that Gabe's phone had no songs on them. I'm guessing the killer thought to erase them too."

I was thrilled that he believed Gabe. "That's a shame. I'll let him know. I called to let you know that last night, I spoke with Carla, his maid."

"And?"

I told him everything she said. "I didn't get the sense she knew much."

"Thanks for the update. By the way, Elissa received the information back on Gabe's tissue sample. She said, his cells were abnormally clean."

"What does that mean?"

"She wouldn't speculate other than to say he wasn't poisoned."

That made sense. "What do you think?"

"That Gabe might really be a super healthy vampire." Steve chuckled.

Too bad I couldn't tell if he believed it or not. "I'll let him know he wasn't poisoned. I'll keep quiet about the fact he might be a vampire."

"You do that." Steve disconnected.

Once I was presentable, I did a quick stop in the bathroom and then came out to three ghosts and Iggy.

"Hi, everyone." I tried to sound as cheerful as possible.

"What did the sheriff say?" Bella asked.

"There were no songs on Gabe's phone. He's guessing the killer erased them too."

"Darn," Gabe said. "I know I can't ever use them, but whoever killed me sure was thorough."

"I agree."

Iggy was on the coffee table, clearly enjoying the attention. "I found out something," he said.

"Is that so? What is it?"

"I was telling everyone that you spoke with Carla. Gabe said that he'd fixed her up with Rod, one of the band members."

I looked over at Gabe. "Is that true?"

"Yes. I would have told you, but I honestly forgot about it."

"Are they still dating?" This might throw off some of my theories.

"No, they broke up two weeks ago."

Shortly before Gabe died. "Had you written the song 'Meet Me Tomorrow' by then?"

"I guess, why?"

Why? Surely, he was smart enough to connect the dots—unless he didn't want to. "Maybe Rod heard that you were writing again and thought he could learn something by dating Carla."

"Rod isn't like that."

I hadn't meant to insult his former band member, but people can and do change. "Maybe it wasn't intentional, but

Carla could have let it slip to Rod about your new endeavor, and he told the band you were getting back into music again. On the other hand, he and Carla might have broken up because they weren't compatible—nothing more."

"I like that theory better," Gabe said.

"Before your most recent call to DMan, when did you last speak with any of your band members?" I had thought there hadn't been any interactions in years.

"Every once in a while, I met DMan for lunch. We're still friends. But no one else."

"I see." That's where the leak might have come from. "Did you talk about your songs with him at lunch?"

"Actually, no. I wanted to have a few done before I told him about my new project. I was feeling him out to see how the band was doing and whether they'd be willing to have me back."

"Since you asked for a meeting with DMan, I take it you thought you'd be welcomed back?" I asked.

"Welcomed? No, but the band was running low on funds. Without additional money, they'd have to fold, which would be hard for most of them. Not everyone is cut out for the nine-to-five type of job."

"In that case, I would think they'd be begging you to return. Having you as their lead singer might help infuse life into the band. After all, The Rebels were named after you."

"I thought the same thing, but clearly, I was wrong."

"We can't be certain one of your band members was responsible. It could have been one of your clients who killed you."

"I know."

Lorenzo moved next to Iggy and faced me. "What would you like us to do today?" he asked me.

"Yesterday, you focused on the band members. Maybe you

should check out Gabe's three irate clients. There are three of you. Nicky found their addresses, and I copied them down."

"You don't want to meet them?" Gabe asked.

He was sweet. "I think that's the sheriff's job. People don't open up to a teenager."

"I bet more than to a law officer," Bella said.

"Perhaps. If Steve needs my help, I will, of course, do what he asks."

My cell rang. When I checked the caller ID, I almost got a chill. "I must be psychic. It's Steve again." I swiped the button. "Yes, Sheriff?"

"Gotta love caller ID. I forgot to mention that I checked Gabe's phone to see if he canceled his appointment with DMan."

"And did he?"

"Yes. Can you ask him why?"

I looked over at Gabe. "He said he didn't cancel. Could his killer have done it after he took out Gabe?"

Steve whistled. "I must be slipping. I hadn't thought of that."

Uh-oh. "While I have you on the line, I, too, forgot to mention Iggy's theory."

"What's that?"

"It's possible the killer erased DMan's memory from when Gabe called him and from when he sang him the song he'd written. It could be why DMan wasn't aware that the song Sev said he wrote really belonged to Gabe."

Steve whistled. "That is quite out there. Any proof?"

"It's hard to prove that someone used magic to erase a person's memory."

"You're right."

"One more thing. I just learned that Carla, Gabe's maid, dated Ron Anderson, one of the band members, for a while.

They only broke up two weeks ago. It's possible that Carla let it leak that Gabe was writing songs again."

"If she was cleaning for a few hours on the weekend, she might have heard Gabe practice," he said.

"That's what I was thinking."

"Even if Carla leaked the information to the band, who stole the music? And was it the same person who harmed Gabe?"

"I hadn't considered that there could be multiple crimes involved, but that makes sense. Is there anything I can help you with?"

"Not at the moment. Keep me informed if you learn anything more."

"I will." I swiped off my phone.

"What did Steve say?" Gabe asked.

"Pretty much nothing other than he checked your phone. Apparently, someone used your phone to cancel your appointment with DMan."

"It had to be the killer—or the person who wanted me out of the way for a while."

"I agree. The big question would be why? This whole stasis thing still seems off to me." Despite the fact I was leaning more toward Lorenzo's theory that Gabe could be vampire. It also meant that the sorcerer must have been able to tell that Gabe was a vampire. Or could a regular person be put into stasis? That might be cool if there were no side effects.

"Unless the person didn't intend to kill Gabe," Lorenzo said.

"And that helps me how?" Gabe asked.

He was right. "It doesn't."

My cell rang. "I'm popular this morning, I see." When I checked the caller ID, I didn't recognize the number. "Hello?"

"Rihanna, this is Elliot Warfel."

Goose bumps raced up my arms. I couldn't guess why he

would be calling. "Hi." I mouthed it was Elliot. "Can I put you on speaker?"

"Sure."

"There are two more ghosts here, but I'm not sure if you can hear them. Don't ask me why, but since you've never met them, you might not be able to."

"No problem."

I clicked on the speaker setting. "Go ahead."

"This morning, Mona stopped by my office. My desk faces the street, which means I can see who comes and goes. Guess who dropped Mona off?"

Playing guessing games wasn't my favorite thing to do. "Who?"

"Kitty."

Gabe lifted an arm to his chest. "My Kitty? As in my former girlfriend, Kitty Fox?"

"The one and only."

I looked over at the others.

"Did you ask Mona how she knew Kitty?" Gabe asked.

"No. We had an appointment to go over what was left of her finances. I didn't want to alert her that someone thought she might be involved in your death. I felt it best to keep it professional."

Gabe shrugged. "You might be right."

"In case you haven't been following the market, Gabe, Cloud 9 has recovered a bit, which is why Mona might not be as upset with you as she was. The movement wasn't enough to make anyone whole, but it's better than when...you know... you died."

"Good to know." Gabe slightly shook his head.

"Anything else?" I asked Elliot.

"Naturally, I wanted to ask Mrs. Leanders if she'd put some kind of voodoo spell on Gabe, but I didn't. She would have only denied it." He kind of chuckled. "I didn't need her to turn on me, if she was guilty."

I wasn't sure if a voodoo spell would work, but it didn't matter. "That was smart. If you speak with the other two clients and they say anything useful, let us know."

"I will."

I disconnected and looked up at Gabe. "What do you think? Are Kitty and Mona related somehow?"

He looked away for a moment, then returned his attention to us. "I have no idea."

How could he not know? "How long did you say you two dated?"

I would have thought they would have discussed each other's parents, or didn't Gabe want to talk about his? Being adopted might have been a sore subject for him.

"On and off for maybe six months. We had a different kind of relationship than most people, I suppose. I was on the road a lot, so our relationship was more of a one-night stand kind of thing. We weren't at the stage where I expected to be invited to dinner to meet the parents, you know what I mean? We never professed our love for each other or anything either."

"That puts things in a new light," Bella said. "Maybe she did kill you. Kitty might have wanted more in the relationship than just a romp in the hay, so to speak."

"Why wait ten years to kill him?" I asked.

"Bella, Bella," Lorenzo said. "Not only what Rihanna said, but there are plenty of women who aren't interested in the house and white picket fence ideal. They want the glamour of being with a player."

"Like you?" she asked.

"Precisely."

I was lucky that Gavin and I weren't like that. I knew Gavin's mom and was there when Gavin found out his father had been murdered. "I should see if Steve can find out about those two."

"Good idea. In the meantime, how about if I spy on Mona, and Lorenzo checks out Kitty?" Bella suggested.

"That's a great idea, but be careful in case she can see you."

Bella kind of planted a hand on her hip. "What can she do to me if she can? Kill me?" Then Bella laughed.

"No, and she won't know who you are even if she could see you, which is a good thing."

"What should I do?" Gabe asked.

"How about hanging back here for a bit? I might need you to help me brainstorm."

"Okay."

I turned to Bella. "Do you need their addresses to find them?" I had no idea how these guys found anyone.

"Nope. We're good." And then they were gone.

Just as I was about to ask Gabe a question, my cell rang. "I never get this many calls in the morning." Then again, I have never tried to solve a crime in Witch's Cove before. I smiled when I saw it was Elissa. "Hey there."

"Steve said he told you about Gabe's tissue sample results?"

"He did." Those two seemed to be in constant contact. "Can you conclude anything from that?"

"Just that Gabe was a very healthy man."

"Not healthy enough apparently."

Elissa cleared her throat. "You're right. I called because I also have the results of the hair that Iggy found in Gabe's house."

So much for filling me in on the tissue stuff. I put her on speaker and motioned Iggy to move closer, not that she could hear him if he spoke. "What kind of dog was it?"

"That's the thing. It wasn't a dog. It was a fox."

I swallowed a laugh. "A fox, as in the wild animal kind of fox?"

"I suppose someone might have a fox as a pet, but they are wild. Iggy needs to be careful around them. They like to eat reptiles."

"Seriously?" Iggy said. "Okay. I'm off this case."

I'd wait until after I finished with my call before I assured him that I wouldn't let anything happen to him.

I looked over at Gabe and then at Iggy, but from their expressions they didn't know who had a fox. "What did Steve say?"

"He had no idea what it meant, which is why he suggested I call you."

"I have no idea either, but if anything comes up, I'll give him a call."

"Good, and Gavin sends his love."

Aw. I adored my boyfriend. "Thanks, Elissa."

When I disconnected, Gabe was eye level with Iggy. "What do you think, Detective Iggy?"

"YOU'RE ASKING *me* about the fact a fox was in *your* house?" Iggy asked.

Gabe nodded. "Yes. I know no one who owns a fox, not unless one of the band members is hiding something."

"Don't look at me. I got nothing."

I chuckled at Iggy's response. "When Bella and Lorenzo return, I'll ask them if they spotted a fox in anyone's home."

"I thought they went out to check on Kitty and Mona," Gabe said.

"I know, but they spent time with the band before that."

"True."

"On the other hand, maybe this fox is like Bandit," Iggy said.

I couldn't figure out what he was talking about. "What do you mean? I know Bandit is very talented at breaking into places, but I doubt he'd have the ability to crawl up the book-case and look through each book. Or are you saying the fox is some owner's familiar?"

"Who's this Bandit?" Gabe asked, before Iggy could answer.

"He's a talking raccoon. He's a familiar like Iggy."

Iggy lifted his chest. "He's more than that."

I'd hurt his feelings. "I know. He's your very smart friend."

Iggy glared at me for a moment and then opened his mouth. "Yes, but I have an idea. What if the fox is a *shifter*?"

"A shifter, huh? Are you saying you've seen a fox shifter?" I asked. "Or that Bandit has seen a fox shifter." There were plenty of foxes in Florida.

"No, but if a stone statue can change into a human and a wolf can change into a human, why can't a fox turn into a human?"

Sure, Kitty's last name was Fox, but I'd known others with the same last name, and I was quite sure they weren't shifters. If fox shifters existed, wouldn't someone have mentioned it by now? Then again, none of us knew gargoyle or vampires existed until recently either.

Gabe flew between us. "Just hold it. Are you saying that things like werewolves really exist?"

If vampires could exist as well as familiars, why not shifters? "Yes. In fact, I know several, though I've only seen Genevieve shift into her statue form once. I know both Glinda and Iggy have watched a group of men shift into wolves."

Gabe faced Iggy. "That true?"

"Yup. You need to get rid of your pre-conceived notions about the world, my friend."

If I had been drinking coffee, I probably would have sprayed it all over my adorable iguana. "Iggy, not all people are fortunate enough to have been born into magic."

Gabe floated away. "I certainly hadn't thought I might have been, or should I say, I had no idea that I had been—assuming Lorenzo is correct in saying I am a vampire."

"I guess we won't know until we ask the person who put the spell on you—assuming that's what really happened."

"True."

"You should tell Steve my idea," Iggy said.

"What do you think Steve can do about it?" Steve was a believer in shifters since his deputy was a wolf shifter, as was the forest ranger, but I bet he would be skeptical that a fox shifter even existed. Maybe if Bandit could shift—or Iggy—we both might be more open.

I glanced over at Gabe. He was facing the window, his shoulders slumped. Gabe seemed a lot more depressed about his death than any of the other ghosts I'd met. He needed cheering up. "Would you like to attend The Rebels' concert tomorrow night?"

He took a moment before turning around. "Would I? Hmm. If I weren't dead, sure, but it might make me sad that I can't be in a band ever again."

That might be a problem. "I think you should go, if only to see if they stole your songs."

His shoulders straightened. "You're right. I will go. Where is it?"

"Let me check the location." Though I didn't think traveling long distances was an issue for a ghost. I went into my room and looked up the concert schedule. When I saw that tickets were still available, I bought two—one for me and one for Nicky. So what if it was at the back of the arena?

I returned to the main office area and told Gabe that the concert started at eight tomorrow. "It's at the Amalie Arena in Tampa."

"Will Bella or Lorenzo know where it is?"

"I don't know, but I'll be driving. You can go with us."

He chuckled. "Thanks. Maybe I'll float up to the stage to see if I can mess with any of them."

"That's not a bad plan. We might be able to find out who is a warlock. However, if one of them is, he would find it difficult to concentrate with a ghost flying back and forth."

Gabe laughed. "That would be fun to see."

"Can I come with you?" Iggy asked.

"I guess, but do you want to?"

"Would I have asked if I didn't?"

"I suppose not." Sometimes I had the sense he only asked to see what I would say.

My cell pinged, and I picked up my phone. "It's from Steve." I read the contents.

"What did it say?" Gabe asked.

"The sheriff in your town asked for the names of those who entered the gate around the time of your death."

"And?"

"No one other than me, Nicky, and Carla visited you."

"Yet someone was inside the house."

"A fox shifter," Iggy said with confidence.

"Of course. A fox shifter. And who would that be, Detective Iggy?" I wasn't ready to discount his theory, but I had no idea how to find such a person.

"I don't know, but we'll figure out a way to set a trap."

I liked that idea. "What kind of trap?"

"You ask a lot of me. You and Glinda get all the glory when I'm the one who solves the crimes."

"Is that so? If I recall, Lorenzo helped solve Bella's murder."

"You know what I mean."

"Yes, I do. When you think of this plan, let me know." I looked at the time. "I'm going to call Nicky and see if she wants to grab some breakfast. What are you two going to do?"

"How about if Gabe and I pay a visit to Bandit?"

"Sure, but I think Gabe would prefer to work on the case."

"This is about the case," Iggy said.

Sometimes talking to him was like pulling teeth—slow and painful. "How so?"

"Bandit wanders about. He might know of a fox who is a shifter."

That was interesting. "Are you saying he can sense if a person is a shifter?"

Iggy looked over at Gabe and then back at me. "I don't know. I've never asked him."

I needed to eat, and Iggy and Gabe might as well have something to do. "Go ahead and visit him. We'll catch up at some point."

"Okay." Iggy turned to Gabe. "Come on. I'll show you the Hex and Bones apothecary. I don't know if you remember Hugo and Genevieve since you were dead at the time and not yet a ghost, but they live there."

"Lead the way."

As soon as those two left, I let out a breath. It was nice to be by myself for a minute. Having ghosts hang around me could be a little overwhelming at times. However, I promised myself that I would help Gabe. I called Nicky and asked if she wanted to meet me at the Tiki Hut Grill.

"Sure. I'll be there as soon as I can."

I smiled. That might mean an hour, which was fine by me. I could always chat with Aunt Fern, assuming she wasn't with a customer.

As I walked over, I glanced up at the monkey bridge that allowed Iggy to cross the street safely. Since I didn't see him, I had to assume he was already in the occult store.

As soon as I entered Aunt Fern's restaurant, my muscles relaxed. I always felt safe and welcomed in there.

When she spotted me, she came out from behind the counter. "How is the search for that nice young man's killer coming?" she asked.

"It's a slow process. Did you hear someone broke into his house and stole his music?"

"I did. Do you know who did it?"

"Since the band was playing one of Gabe's songs recently,

someone in the band is probably guilty." I told her about the fox hairs. "Have you ever heard of a fox shifter?"

"Not a fox exactly, but I've heard of a bird shifter. That's about as odd an animal that I can recall."

A bird shifter? I wouldn't mind having that talent. I could fly wherever I wanted. "Did Pearl or any of the other ladies give you any good gossip?"

She leaned closer. "Maude said that Arnie Driscoll seemed the happiest he'd been in a while now that Gabe is dead. Apparently, Gabe was the financial advisor who lost Arnie a lot of money."

"I heard Arnie borrowed the money for the investment from his brother."

Aunt Fern nodded. "The whole thing is so tragic."

"It is. Anything else?"

"Not at the moment, but I'll let you know if I learn anything."

"Thanks." I looked around and spotted Penny. "I'll sit in Penny's section."

"Sure."

"I'm expecting my friend Nicky to join me."

"I'll send her over."

I found a table in Penny's section. Since she was dating the forest ranger who was a werewolf, she might know something about a fox shifter—or so I hoped.

As soon as she finished with her customer, she came over. "Hi, Rihanna. Have you heard from Glinda?"

"No, but they don't have Internet or cell service in the woods, so I can't contact her. I wish I could."

"I worry about her. She's not the outdoorsy type."

I chuckled. "I think that is why Jaxson wanted her to go. I bet he's hoping to change her mind."

Penny smiled. "I wish him luck."

Now came for the hard question. I looked around to make

sure no one was close enough to hear. "Have you ever heard of a fox shifter?"

She pressed her lips together. "I'd have to ask Hunter. He might have. Why?"

"Long story, but it looks as if a fox shifter might have broken into Gabe's house—he's the man who died." I explained about the fox hairs Iggy found in the living room.

"I heard about his death. But how would any kind of shifter open a door?"

"I figured this person entered the gated community as a fox and then changed into his or her human form." But then there wouldn't be any hair inside the house. Darn. Unless..." Let me ask you something. When you-know-who *changes* back, does he still have any of his animal hair on him?"

"Too often. Thankfully, he's not in his other form a lot."

"That's helpful."

Nicky came in the restaurant, and I waved to her. "That's my friend."

Penny waited until Nicky was seated. "I got here as fast as I could."

"I was just giving Penny the rundown on the case. She and Glinda are best friends."

"Oh. I see." Nicky introduced herself and then shook Penny's hand.

"Coffee?"

"That would be great," I said.

Since Penny had walked over with the pot, she poured us some. "I'll give you a minute to decide what you want."

"Thanks."

"Did you learn anything new?" Nicky asked.

"I think so." I told her about the phone calls from Elliot, Elissa, and Steve. I didn't mention that Penny would speak with her boyfriend about a possible fox shifter, since Hunter didn't want people to know he was a werewolf.

"What about our ghost friends?"

"Bella is checking out Mona, Lorenzo is following Kitty, and Iggy and Gabe are speaking with Bandit." I explained Iggy's theory about a fox shifter.

"My mind is blown. I had no idea there were fox shifters."

"We can't be sure there are. It's just a guess." I lifted my coffee cup. "And I bought tickets to the concert tomorrow."

"Great! I can't wait."

"Gabe—and I'm sure the others—will go with us. I'd like to find out if the band performs any of Gabe's new songs. He'll know for sure."

"Good plan. That will narrow down the guilty party. Kind of."

"I hope so," I said.

Penny came over and took our order.

"What's next on the agenda?" Nicky asked once Penny headed back to place our order with the kitchen.

"That's what we need to figure out!"

chapter
fifteen

NICKY and I had already returned to the office when Iggy came in with Bandit right behind him while Gabe just floated through the wall.

"Hello, Bandit. This is a nice surprise," I said.

"Hey." He glanced over at Iggy and then turned back to us. "I can't believe Iggy practically solved Gabe's murder case by himself and never asked for my help."

"Is that so?" Iggy didn't often stretch the truth that much. He must be missing Glinda a lot.

"I can see you don't believe me, but remember I was the one who knew a fox was somehow involved. If you recall, Genevieve said there were animal prints outside of that broken-down farm house where we found Gabe."

I had completely forgotten about that. "You're right." I turned to Bandit. "Have you met a fox shifter?"

"I've seen quite a few foxes. I've never seen them shift into a human before my eyes, though."

That was kind of disappointing.

"Can you tell if someone is a shifter?" I asked.

"Sure. Or most of the time I can. I'm just not good at knowing what they can shift into though."

"Iggy, you can't, can you?"

"You know I can't, just like you witches can't tell if someone is a witch."

"Touché. Bandit, who in Witch's Cove is a shifter?"

He looked over at Iggy. "She's a sly one. She's trying to trick me. You know Nash Solano is a shifter as is Penny's boyfriend. To be honest, I never would have figured out that Genevieve and Hugo were gargoyle shifters. I think my talents only extend to the human kind of shifters."

And both Genevieve and Hugo were originally made from stone. "I get it." A crazy idea struck me. "You know, it would be cool if Gabe could take you back stage tomorrow night at The Rebels' concert. You might be able to figure out who is a shifter."

Before he answered, Iggy looked up at me. "What about me?"

"Bandit can keep cloaked longer than you. The concert could last hours."

"It takes effort on Bandit's part to stay cloaked too. We should ask Hugo to take us. He can hold us both since we don't weigh much."

If Iggy sat on Hugo's shoulder while Hugo held the larger raccoon, it might be okay. "How about I call Genevieve and ask her to ask Hugo?"

"Great," Iggy said.

I looked over at Bandit. "You up for a little sleuthing?"

"Does garbage smell?"

I laughed and pulled out my phone. I called Genevieve and explained the situation.

"When do you need us?"

I hadn't thought Genevieve would want to come, but then Bandit was their adopted familiar. "Tomorrow at seven thirty? That will give you time to explore the area."

"That works. We'll stop by then to pick up Iggy."

"Thank you."

I disconnected and told everyone the plan.

"All you need to know is whether one of the four band members is a shifter, right?" Bandit asked.

Was that all? "Yes, and if you hear anyone cheer about Gabe's death, that will be good, too, even though Gabe will be with you. It's possible, you might decide to divide and conquer. We'll have Bella and Lorenzo there too. I'll let Gabe decide who needs to be with whom."

Bandit looked over at Iggy. "This will be so much fun. I haven't worked on a case since the Pink Moon Rising movie company came to town."

That was when one of the cast members in the movie had been murdered—Bandit's host in fact. I guess he'd recovered from his loss, though Glinda said the host wasn't the best person to have a familiar.

"What should we do until then?" Bandit asked.

"I'm not sure. I'm going to do some brainstorming with Nicky and Gabe. You two go have fun."

Iggy crawled over to me and looked up. "Are you implying we can't brainstorm?"

I hadn't meant to insult him. "Not at all. I didn't think you'd enjoy it."

"We'll stay."

"Okay. Bella and Lorenzo are with two of Gabe's clients."

"Maybe I should check out Pamela Vetters. I did say it could be any of the three," Gabe said.

"How about helping us for a bit, and then you can go?"

"Okay."

"Let me get my laptop so I can take notes."

I went into my bedroom, grabbed my computer, and returned. I sat on the sofa next to Nicky. Gabe floated in front of us, while Iggy climbed onto his favorite spot on the coffee table. Bandit moved next to the chair across from the sofa.

I opened a Word document. "Gabe, can you list the new songs you recently wrote? I want to see if they play any of them." Not that Gabe wouldn't know and tell us.

"I figure they would try. Why else take them?"

"I don't know."

Gabe listed his songs. He had enough to make an album, which was sad in a way since he'd never have the chance to perform them.

"Did you ask Steve if there was a relationship between Kitty Fox and Mona Leanders?" Nicky asked.

I hissed in a breath. "I forgot." Forgetfulness seemed to be in the air.

"Do it now," she urged.

"Okay, okay." I called Steve and explained that when Mona Leanders visited Elliot for financial advice, it was Kitty who'd dropped her off. "Could you find out how they know each other?"

"Are you wondering if they work together or if they are related, or what?"

"All of the above?"

Steve chuckled. "Too bad Jaxson is out of town. I often rely on him to do the deep dive."

"I know. Oh, by the way, a group of us are heading to Tampa tomorrow to see The Rebels perform."

"I'm sure you'll enjoy it, but do you have an ulterior motive?"

"Yes. Gabe and I want to know if the band plays any of Gabe's songs. If they do, it means one of them stole the music."

"Good thinking. Do you really think the theft would warrant killing someone? Gabe was willing to return to the band," Steve said.

"Seems to me whoever took the songs didn't want Gabe to return."

"Could be. Let me know how the concert is, and I'll see if there is a connection between Kitty Fox and Mona Leanders. Do you know Kitty's full name? It is Katherine?"

"Let me ask Gabe." I motioned him over. "Do you know Kitty's full name."

"I never asked her."

"Ouch."

Gabe shrugged. "Sorry."

"No skin off my back." I told Steve that Gabe didn't know.

"I'll see what I can find out."

"Oh, I forgot to ask, did the sheriff where Gabe lives find anything useful in his house—like fingerprints or anything?"

Nicky leaned close. "My fingerprints are going to be everywhere."

"I heard that," Steve said. "What's Nicky's full name?"

"Nicole Andrews."

"When you have a moment, maybe you two could stop over and give me your prints. I can send them over to the sheriff so he can eliminate yours."

"We'll do that."

He then disconnected.

"Steve is on the case. He asked if we could stop over at his office and be fingerprinted, so the sheriff over where Gabe lives can eliminate our prints."

She blew out a breath. "That's a good idea."

I snapped my fingers. "I should call Elliot and ask him to do a little digging on Pamela Vetters. If she hasn't contacted him already, maybe he can find out if she's happy or sad that Gabe is dead."

"She won't be crying," Gabe announced.

"Probably not. I don't expect her to state her opinion, but I bet Elliot can judge her mood." I called him and asked if he could check her out. I told Elliot I wanted to be thorough in looking into all of the people Gabe thought might have killed him. Yes, it was the sheriff's job, but Elliot, being a warlock, might sense things better than Steve.

"Sure. I was planning on calling her tomorrow anyway."

"Great. I appreciate it." I disconnected and then turned to Nicky. "How about we get those fingerprints done?"

"Let's do it."

I looked around the Amalie Arena where the first band was warming up. Apparently, five bands would be playing several original songs each in order to compete for a fifty-thousand-dollar prize. That might be enough motive to kill Gabe.

Nicky leaned over. "It's no wonder they wanted Gabe's songs. If the band is doing so poorly, this might be their only chance to survive."

Had she read my mind? It was kind of creepy when other people knew what I was thinking. "Since Gabe is a great artist, his songs might be just what they needed."

Her eyes widened. "If we assume—and that's a stretch—that Gabe is a vampire and someone put him in stasis, do you think they planned on taking him out of this stasis state after the competition?"

"I have no idea. I should ask Lorenzo if he knows what a vampire remembers after coming out of stasis. Had Gabe not died for real, he might not even know that time had passed," I said.

The lights dimmed and the audience hushed. An emcee came on stage and asked us to welcome Starfire. I must not listen much to popular music since I hadn't heard of them either.

For the next two hours, we listened to the other four bands. Unfortunately for me, The Rebels were the last to perform, so I had to sit through all of the music. Some were good. Others? Not so much. Hopefully, our ghosts, familiars, and shifters would learn a lot during their time backstage.

When The Rebels were introduced, I took out my phone. I wanted to record a few seconds of each song. The first one seemed to be about meeting someone tomorrow. I leaned over to Nicky. "That's Gabe's song."

"I like it."

So far, each band had played five songs. Apparently, the judges would rate the top two songs that each group played, and then give the monetary reward to the winner. No one mentioned a record deal, but I wouldn't be surprised if that might be part of it.

I had to say that The Rebels' first song was very moving. Did I think Sev did a great job singing it? Not particularly, but the others provided much-needed backup. I partially recorded each of their songs. I didn't know if the other four songs were written by Gabe, but they were nice. Was the band worthy of winning the prize? Not in my opinion.

Turns out the judges agreed with me. They went through the reasons for their decision. They basically said that The Rebels' songs were excellent, but the execution could have been better, which most likely hurt Sev's ego. I bet now he wished he'd welcomed Gabe into the band. They might have won the contest if Gabe had been the lead singer.

Once the concert was over, people poured out of the arena, all chatting about whether they agreed with the judges or not. I couldn't wait to hear what our spies had to say.

I nudged Nicky. "Look, there's Kitty. She's going backstage."

"Wouldn't she need a pass?"

"I'm sure the band is given a few to hand out."

We slowly made our way to the exit. As much as I wanted to hear what gossip they'd picked up, no one needed a ride home. In fact, I wouldn't be surprised if everyone was back at the office long before us. Bandit was nocturnal, and neither of the gargoyle shifters or the ghosts needed to sleep. The only one who might be tired would be Iggy.

The drive home took about ninety minutes, and it was almost two in the morning before we arrived. Since we knew we'd be late, I had suggested Nicky spend the night on the couch in the living room, and she was fine with that.

When we traipsed up the stairs, everyone was there. Except for Hugo, I think they all spoke at once.

"Hold it," I said. "One at a time."

chapter
sixteen

I LOOKED AT GABE. "Why don't you start?"

Iggy shook his head, clearly unhappy that I hadn't asked the all-knowing iguana to begin.

"They played three of my songs. Three! Not that I can use them, but when Sev got up there and announced that he'd written them, I wanted to wring his neck."

I was surprised he didn't ask Hugo to temporarily do something to him. Gabe probably didn't because he really wanted to see if his songs were good enough to win the prize.

"How did the band react to the loss?" I asked.

Bella flew to the front. "There were a lot of people around, but DMan was displeased with Sev that he sang off key or something."

He sounded kind of bad to me at times too.

"The group was very disappointed they didn't win. Sev, in particular, acted guilty," Lorenzo said. "He paced and didn't make a lot of eye contact with the group."

Iggy looked over at Hugo and then back at me and Nicky. "Hugo wanted to do his magic on each of them to see if they were telling the truth, but there wasn't an opportunity. He might be able to cloak himself, but if he placed his hands on the sides of their heads to gather their thoughts, they'd feel it."

"I see."

"Do you think that the band believes that Sev wrote those songs? They were awesome, by the way, Gabe."

"Thank you, Rihanna. I don't know what they thought. My music is nothing like what Sev has written, but maybe he told them he needed to change his style."

Nicky leaned closer. "What about Kitty? Do you think she believed Sev when he said the songs were his? Or do we think she had something to do with the theft?"

Bandit hopped up on the coffee table next to Iggy. That was the first time I'd seen him do that. "She knew."

"You know this how?" I asked.

"She is a shifter."

"What? Are you sure?" I asked.

"I can sense these things. Do I know if she's a fox shifter? No. I'd suggest one of the ghosts keep watch on her, but she might only shift when it's really necessary."

"That makes sense."

Iggy waddled closer to me. "Why don't you ask Nash Solano? Being a werewolf and all, he might be able to sense what kind of shifter someone is."

"Who is Nash Solano?" Nicky asked.

"He's our deputy, but please don't say anything. It's not something he wants other people to know about."

She nodded. "My lips are sealed."

"I'll text the sheriff tomorrow. Nash could interview Kitty about something and decide if she is one or not—assuming he can tell."

"What about the paw prints behind the farm house?" Iggy asked. "You should ask Hunter about that. As a forest ranger, he'd know what kind of animal it is."

"Yes, he would. Sometimes you surprise me."

"Surprise you?" Iggy blew out of his mouth, but it didn't make much of a sound. I assumed it was supposed to be a harrumph.

"What else did you guys pick up?" I asked.

"I think a band member did me in," he said.

"I would agree except for one tiny fact: which of the band members has the power to put you in stasis—assuming that's what happened? I'm not saying you are or aren't a vampire, but whoever did it would need to be able to wield a lot of power."

Lorenzo moved closer. "Putting someone into a trance might not be extremely difficult, but taking them out would require a very powerful sorcerer. And we're not talking about an ordinary witch—no offense to our two lovely witches."

"No offense taken," I said.

"If one of the band members was that powerful, he should have put a spell on the judges to make them give the band the award," Bella said.

I chuckled. "You might be right."

"I'm sorry, Gabe, that I picked that farm house to take pictures of," Nicky said. "If I hadn't, you might be alive today."

"Bad luck, I guess, but I'm not so sure the band would have brought me back to life," he said.

That was something I had been wondering about. "Why? Because if they'd won the award, they wouldn't need you anymore?"

"Exactly."

But they lost. Perhaps they hadn't anticipated that would happen. I yawned. "How about we reconvene tomorrow? After a good night's sleep, I might come up with a plan."

"Okay," Bella said, and then the ghosts disappeared.

Bandit jumped down off the table. "I'll try to think of

something. Between my two hosts and me, we should be able to come up with something."

"That would be nice. Goodnight, Bandit. And thanks for your help."

He nodded and hightailed it out the door. I stood. "I'm hitting the hay. Nicky, let me get you some blankets and a pillow."

The next morning, I texted Steve about the fact that Bandit believed Kitty Fox might be a fox shifter—and no, it wasn't because of her name. In case he hadn't researched her, I told him where she worked.

My phone rang a minute later. It was Steve. "Hello, that was fast," I said.

"I've been up for a while. I wanted to touch base to let you know that I did a little research on Kitty Fox and Mona Leanders. They are related."

"How?"

"Mother and daughter. Mona used to be Mona Fox. When her husband died, she remarried Doug Leanders."

"Unlucky lady to be a widow twice."

"I thought that too," he said. "I plan to ask both ladies to come in for questioning. I want to fingerprint them and compare the prints to those at Gabe's house."

"That's awesome." We might actually be one step closer to solving the case.

"How was the concert, by the way? Learn anything?"

"Beside Bandit claiming Kitty is a shifter and the fact that the band played three of Gabe's new songs at the concert?"

"Yes."

"Sev announced that *he'd* written the songs."

"Interesting."

I wasn't surprised that Steve wouldn't speculate about who took the music. "I forgot to mention that the concert was really a competition." I explained about the prize money. "They didn't win."

"I trust you're thinking the song theft was about increasing the band's chance of winning the award?" he asked.

"Yes. If Gabe had been invited to join them, that would have meant less money for each of them."

"I'll make a note of the possible motive for murder," Steve said.

"Great. Iggy suggested we ask Hunter if the prints behind the farm house belonged to a fox."

"I already called him."

That was one less item for me to be concerned about. "Anything you need me to do?"

"If you can figure out who has the ability to put a spell on poor Gabe, that would go a long way to closing this case."

I laughed. "Sure thing. Why didn't I think of that?"

Uh-oh. I'd been hanging out around Bella too much. My sarcasm had returned. Once I disconnected, I quickly changed and went out to the living room.

The water was running in the shower, but Iggy was wandering around.

"About time you got up. I'm hungry," he said.

"Sorry." I quickly fixed him a plate of lettuce. "What's on your agenda today?"

"You are so funny."

"I guess it's up to me to solve the case then."

"You wish," Iggy said.

I couldn't help but smile. "Have you seen our ghost friends?"

"No, but I bet they are scoping out the band members."

"Good."

Nicky came out of the bathroom. "Are we going to solve the case today?" she asked.

"Why do people think I know?" I inhaled. "However, I need to adopt a more positive attitude, so yes. Maybe."

Nicky smiled. "How about some breakfast brainstorming time?"

"Works for me. The diner?"

"My thoughts exactly."

Iggy was moving toward his exit. "Are you going someplace?" I asked.

"Bandit, Hugo, and I will figure things out."

"You do that."

My cell rang, and I checked the caller ID. "It's Elliot Warfel again," I told her. "Hello, Elliot."

"Rihanna. I wanted to bring you up to speed on Pamela Vetters."

"Can I put you on speaker? Nicky is here."

"Sure."

"Go ahead."

"When I asked if she was interested in me taking over her finances, she said she had no more money."

"Ouch," I said.

"Exactly. Apparently, Pamela and her husband were living off their dividends from other stock purchases, but that wasn't enough for Pamela. Behind her husband's back, she decided to invest the money she'd been saving for their daughter's college into this Cloud 9 get-rich-quick scheme."

"And she lost her money." I felt sorry for her.

"Yes. As a result, she and her husband were unable to pay their mortgage payments and other bills, so they had to move into a smaller place. Needless to say, the daughter will not be going to college any time soon either."

"I trust the husband was unhappy about this? Or was the daughter more upset?"

"She didn't say, but her life now isn't good. I tried to get a feel for whether she wanted revenge against Gabe or not."

"And?" I asked.

"She said that Gabe had warned her about the risks, but she invested anyway. Pamela never told Gabe where the money was coming from since she feared he'd counsel her against the investment."

I tried to figure out what he meant. "Are you saying that she's accepted her fate, or is she out for blood?"

"I had the sense she has a lot more to worry about than getting back at Gabe."

I imagined she did. "Thanks for your input."

"Any news on who might have killed Gabe?"

I gave him a brief rundown of the concert. "I'll shoot you a text when we learn more."

"I'd appreciate it."

We disconnected, and I turned to Nicky. "Ready to chow?"

"Totally."

When we reached the sidewalk, Iggy was nowhere in sight. I liked how focused he was on this case. It was almost as if he thought of it as a race to see who learned more.

On the short walk over to the diner, I explained to Nicky what Steve told me, including the fact he planned to finger-print both Mona and Kitty.

"That puts a new spin on things," Nicky said.

"How so?" I had my ideas, but I wanted to hear her opinion.

"If my mom had lost her money due to someone's incompetence, I'd want revenge."

"Remind me not to upset you."

Nicky smiled. "I promise not to put you into stasis anytime soon."

"Good luck trying. I just wish we could tell who had the

ability." I lifted a finger. "Before we take on that challenge, we should find out who actually stole the songs."

"My money is on Kitty," Nicky said. "We know a fox was in Gabe's house. If Bandit is right, and Kitty is a fox shifter, it puts her at the scene of the second crime. I'm guessing she stole the songs after Gabe was in his stasis form. Otherwise, he would have found his place turned upside down."

"I agree. I'm hoping that once Steve takes her fingerprints, we'll know the truth."

"Gabe said he didn't tell anyone in the band about having written new material, but could he have said something to Kitty? I know they aren't dating, but maybe they ran into each other somewhere, and he let it slip."

I was impressed with Nicky's insight. "We'll have to ask him."

We entered the Spellbound Diner and grabbed the last available booth. Dolly finished what she was doing and came over. "Howdy, girls. How's the murder investigation coming?"

"The sheriff is working on it," I said.

"Oh, pooh. You are too. I heard you had some ghost help." Dolly grinned. "With that kind of firepower, you could learn a lot."

"That's true. Have you picked up any interesting gossip?"

"Not much, other than the songs the band played at their concert weren't written by the band," Dolly said.

Oh, my. That news traveled fast. "I know." I explained that Gabe's house had been broken into and his music stolen.

She shook her head. "That's terrible. I guess they figured he wasn't needing those songs where he was going."

"I know, but it's still a theft."

Dolly nodded. "True. What can I get you girls?"

Once we ordered, my mind started spinning. I turned my attention back to Nicky. "Like everyone's been saying, the key to the case is finding out who has the power to put a person into stasis and take them out of it."

"How do you plan on finding that out?" she asked.

"Ask the one person who might know—Gertrude Poole." I explained who she was and why she might know.

"I say we visit her."

After we ate and paid, we walked over to the Psychic's Corner where Gertrude worked. She was ancient, but she managed to make it into work all the time. It was strange how she was always there when Glinda needed her. Perhaps she was just psychic enough to know when people were about to book an appointment.

The receptionist told us that Gertrude was free. How coincidental. Even if I asked Gertrude about her ability to always be present, I bet she wouldn't admit anything. Gertrude was cagey like that.

I knocked on her office door, and when she told me to enter, I pushed it open only to find Gertrude bending over the table pouring iced tea into *three* glasses. That kind of creeped me out.

"Rihanna, how nice to see you. And who is your friend?"

Like she didn't know? "Nicky Andrews, a fellow photographer and witch."

"Ah, yes. You two found Gabe Rebel's body."

Was there anything she didn't know? Though to be honest, Iggy had found the body. Nicky never actually saw him. We both sat down. "Any idea who might have killed him?" I asked.

chapter
seventeen

"NOW WHERE WOULD the fun be in that if I told you?"
Gertrude winked.

Since she had helped train me to read minds, she opened
hers to me now. Fortunately, she was just pulling my leg. I
grinned. "None at all."

"What can I help you with?" Gertrude asked.

Since I wasn't sure how much she really knew, I gave her a
brief rundown of what happened. "The sticking point here is
who might be a strong enough witch or warlock to do something like this to Gabe."

"If the witches—or sorcerers—are not from around here, I
probably wouldn't know them."

I hadn't thought of that. "Is there a way to find out, other
than asking around?"

"I can't tell who is an ordinary witch—not that witches
such as you two are ordinary—but if this person is that powerful, I might be able to sense it. That would require me to be
near them, however."

"Steve plans to bring in both mother and daughter for
fingerprinting. How about if I have Hugo cloak you and take
you to the same room as these two people? Might you be able

to tell then?"

"It's possible."

As much as I wanted to pump my fist, I refrained. "If you would be willing to give it a try, that would be great."

She smiled. "Just let me know when, and I'll be ready."

"Great. I'll send Hugo over when the time is right." I stood. "How much do we owe you?" Glinda always paid.

She waved a hand. "For my prize student? Nothing, though I think you knew that."

I chuckled, not knowing what to say, so I waved and left. I doubted I was her prize student anymore since I hadn't studied under Gertrude in quite a while.

"Are you going to tell your sheriff what you plan to do?" Nicky asked.

"I think I'll speak with Hugo first. I'm sure he'll be okay with it, but I want to ask." I pulled out my phone and texted the sheriff to see if he knew when the ladies were due to come in for questioning and have their fingerprints taken.

By the time we reached the Hex and Bones store, I received a text back. I smiled. "Steve is a fast worker. The women will be there in an hour."

"Maybe they have nothing to hide," Nicky said.

"That's probably what they want Steve to think."

Nicky's eyes widened. "When did you become so cynical?"

"I think ever since I met Bella."

She laughed and pulled open the store door. The inside smelled of incense and some kind of strawberry-lemon fragrance. There were a lot of candles in the store, which probably added to the pleasing aroma. I inhaled, letting the sweet scent soothe me. "Let's find Hugo."

Wherever Hugo was, Iggy would be close by. Andorra, one of the owner's granddaughters who often helped with Glinda's cases, came over.

"Iggy is in the back with Hugo and Bandit, if you're looking for him."

I waited for her to say Gabe was with them, but she might think I'd assume that, though it was possible she couldn't see them. "I am. I haven't seen you much of late. How's business?"

"Actually, very good. It's been crazy busy. Even Drake has been complaining that we don't go out as much."

"It has to be hard with both of you being business owners."

"Totally, but I won't be an owner—or part owner—until my grandmother retires."

I hoped for Glinda's sake, as well as mine, that it was never. "I need to ask Hugo a favor."

"Sure. Go ahead."

Nicky and I went into the back room. Besides the four people—assuming I could consider Gabe a person—was Genevieve.

She smiled. "Hey, you two. Iggy, Bandit, and Gabe have been telling us all about what's new with the case."

Hopefully, their information was accurate. "That's why we're here."

"How can we help?" Genevieve asked.

I explained that since Mona Leanders was Kitty Fox's mother, one of them might be powerful enough to have put Gabe into stasis. "Gertrude thinks that if she is close to them, she might be able to assess their abilities. Hugo, could you cloak the two of you and escort Gertrude to the sheriff's conference room or wherever Steve plans to interrogate them?"

He smiled and nodded.

"I can go with them and translate," Iggy said.

"I don't think anyone will be talking when they are inside. I'm hoping it won't take long either."

"Sounds good," Genevieve said. "What time is this interrogation?"

"If Hugo could pick up Gertrude at the Psychics Corner in forty-five minutes and teleport her to the sheriff's office, that would be great."

"Can do," she said.

"What can Bandit, Gabe, and I do?" Iggy asked.

I had to think about that. "In theory, Kitty can't see Gabe. If we assume Mona is that powerful, she might be able to see ghosts."

"Suppose she can?" Gabe said. "I would think it would make her tell the truth. I should be there."

"If you want to go with Hugo and Gertrude, go ahead."

Iggy crawled over to me. "We want to help too."

"Stay here with me. When Hugo returns, we can figure out our next step."

"That gives us an hour." He turned his back to me. "Come on, Bandit, let's explore."

I saw no reason to stop him. Nicky and I sat down to wait.

"Since we have time, I want to call Carla," I said.

"Why?"

"Now that I know she dated one of the band members, I can't help but think she mentioned Gabe was writing songs again."

Nicky sat there for a moment. "You want to know where the leak came from?"

"Exactly. It may not get us any closer to learning who killed Gabe, but I would like to know how the leak occurred."

She smiled. "Go for it."

Since I had Carla's number in my phone, I called her. It rang quite a while before she picked up. "Hello?"

She sounded out of breath, like she was in the middle of cleaning someone's house. I reminded her that I had notified her of Gabe's death. "Could I ask you a question?"

"Sure."

"I heard you dated Rod Anderson for a while."

"I did, but we're not together anymore. If you're wondering if he had anything to do with Gabe's death, he didn't."

She sounded very confident. "Why is that?"

"He wanted Gabe to rejoin the band. While Rod didn't like Sev's singing, he said Gabe's replacement had a good sense for business and was a benefit to the group."

That was interesting. "I'll be sure to mention that to the sheriff. I called to see if by any chance you happened to mention anything to Rod or the other band members about Gabe writing again?"

Carla was silent for a moment. "I've been going over my conversations with Rob ever since I found out about Gabe. I might have mentioned it to him since I knew he'd have been happy to hear that."

"Did Rod ask if Gabe planned to come back to the band?"

"He asked, but I told him I didn't know. He then asked me to snoop in Gabe's house to see how many songs he'd written and to ask Gabe what his intentions were regarding coming back to the band. I couldn't do it. I'd been with Gabe for eleven years and with Rod for less than a month. Since it was none of my business to butt into Gabe's affairs, I told Rod he should ask Gabe himself. That's when I decided we couldn't be together."

"I see. Thank you, Carla, for telling me."

"Is that all?"

"Do you have anything you'd like to add?" I mentally crossed my fingers.

"No."

"Thanks again." I disconnected and told Nicky what Carla said.

"Carla seems innocent of all of this then. She just

happened to be talking about her boss to her boyfriend since the two used to work together," Nicky said.

"That's my take. At least we know how the information was leaked."

After waiting around for an hour, Nicky slumped back in her chair. "What is taking them so long?"

She sounded like I felt. "I bet it's not easy to detect the level of a person's abilities. No one I know—other than Gertrude—could tell whether a person has such sorcerer-level type of witch powers."

I had just uttered that phrase when the contingent of three appeared in the back room of the store. Hugo instantly helped Gertrude over to a seat, and Gabe floated over to the side.

"Well?" I asked.

She smiled. "That was a trip, as you young people say."

"Was either Kitty or Mona a sorcerer?"

"Definitely. The power swirling around in the room was strong."

"Which one was it?" I asked.

"Mona."

"Mona? My money had been on Kitty." I looked over at Gabe. "Could Mona see you?"

"If she could, she didn't say anything, not that I blame her. If Mona put me into stasis, she should be scared now that I'm dead since no one can be positive what the dead know—or might divulge. Too bad, I don't know much."

"She has to know that since you are dead, it would make her a murderer instead of merely a sorcerer who planned to do only a little bit of harm."

"I wish I'd been there," Nicky said. "I could have detected her heart rate to see how scared she was."

"I bet it was high," I threw in.

"How does this help us?" Gabe asked. "Sure, I can put

odds on Mona wanting to keep me out of the way for a while, but how do we prove it?"

"Did Steve take their fingerprints?"

"He did," Gabe said.

"Hugo, why don't you escort Gertrude back to her office?" He nodded. "Gertrude, you have been an invaluable help."

She smiled. "Always happy to be of service."

One moment Gertrude and Hugo were there, and the next, they weren't. I stood. "Field trip to the sheriff's office anyone?"

Genevieve held up a hand. "It might be better if Hugo and I stay here. We don't want to upset the sheriff more than necessary. He's not a big fan of us doing something that isn't within the law."

She was so cool. "Thanks." I looked at Gabe and Nicky. "Ready gang?"

"What should I tell Iggy and Bandit when they return?" Genevieve asked.

"Just what Gertrude told us. If he's finished playing around, Iggy should return to the office."

"Got it."

We left the store, turned left, and walked the one block to the sheriff's office. Inside, Pearl was at the reception desk with a pile of what looked like peanut butter cookies on her desk.

"We have some news about Gabe's case. May we speak with Steve?"

"Sure. You know where his office is."

Boy did I.

I knocked, and the three of us went in. Steve looked up. "I have no information to impart," he said. "I took the women's fingerprints and asked a few questions. Neither confessed to anything."

"I figured, but we have something to tell you."

His eyebrows rose. "Have a seat then."

I explained that Hugo had cloaked himself and Gertrude. "We didn't tell you since we didn't want you to say it was a dumb idea." Or an illegal one.

"Rihanna, you should know by now that I don't think magic is dumb. Please continue."

"I stand corrected. Gertrude was close enough to Mona and Kitty for Gertrude to tell who possibly put Gabe into stasis."

His raised eyebrows implied he was impressed. "It was Kitty, right?"

"No, it was Mona."

"The mom?"

"Yes. Bella once explained to me that it takes many, many years of practice to hone the skill of magic—especially one that powerful."

"Like her grandmother from New Orleans."

"Yes, though she is into voodoo more than straight magic. I don't know enough to say if there is an overlap."

"Got it. Do you believe Mona is responsible for Gabe's death?"

I looked over at Gabe. "What do you think?"

Steve cleared his throat. "I forgot he's been coming in with you lately."

I flashed him a quick smile.

"It's possible," Gabe said. "I basically bankrupted Mona, and her daughter's boyfriend, Sev, might not take kindly to me replacing him. So, yes, she is the best candidate."

I explained that to Steve.

"I sent their digital fingerprints over to the sheriff in Gabe's town, but it will take him a bit to compare them to those found at the crime scene. I do have a question for you. Do you know if Mona needed to touch Gabe in order to put him into this trance-stasis?"

"I'd have to ask Lorenzo."

"He's not here?"

"No. He and Bella are with the band to see if they can pick up any gossip."

Steve leaned back in his chair. "I wish I could see ghosts and have a few ghost deputies. They could come in handy."

He was kidding—or at least I thought he was—though I bet if ghost testimony was admissible in court, he'd ask for a few. The fact they could never be hurt, didn't need to sleep or eat, and could eavesdrop without being seen, would be a huge crime solving benefit. Not to mention, they didn't need to be paid.

Just then Bella and Lorenzo showed up. "Speak of the devils. What did you two find out?" And how did they know where to find us? If I had to guess, they probably tried the office, a few of the restaurants, and then came here. Bella had told me she was fast.

"It was Rod who told Sev about Gabe writing again."

"What did Sev say?" I asked.

Nicky scooted closer to Steve and translated.

"He asked Kitty to steal the songs," Bella said.

"I bet she didn't need any more incentive than her boyfriend asking her to steal, and the fact Gabe nearly bankrupted her mom."

"Thanks, Rihanna. Way to rub it in," Gabe said.

"Sorry."

Once Nicky told Steve what was said, he jotted it down. "Anything else?" he asked.

"No one said anything about Gabe dying, if that's what you want to know," Bella said.

Once Nicky translated, he nodded. "Got it."

"Steve, did Nash have a chance to see if Kitty was a fox shifter?" I nodded to Nicky. "She knows but promises to keep his secret."

He glanced at Nicky and tossed her a half smile. "As a matter of fact, Nash was in the room when I questioned the two women. He said one of them was definitely a shifter. Since the women were sitting next to each other, he couldn't be positive which one was. He didn't sense both were."

"Could he tell if she was a *fox* shifter though?"

chapter
eighteen

"**YES,** Nash can tell if someone is a fox shifter, but only because a fox is similar to his kind," Steve said. "Wolves are members of the Canidae family, which includes wolves and foxes."

"Since we found fox hair in Gabe's house, do you think she stole the songs?"

"Kitty is my top suspect for having broken into Gabe's home after he died, but I need to wait for the sheriff's report. Even if we find her prints in the house, I wouldn't be surprised if she claimed that since she and Gabe had dated that he told her if anything happened to him that she could have the songs."

"I said no such thing," Gabe said.

Nicky repeated what Gabe said.

"I figured. The problem is that no one can hear you regarding your claim, Gabe."

"It stinks that I'm dead."

"For sure," I said.

Lorenzo floated next to Gabe. "There are some benefits to being like us."

"Oh, yeah? Like what?"

"For one, you can hang out with me and Bella whenever you want. And it costs nothing to enjoy yourself. We don't eat, and we don't need a place to sleep."

Gabe chuckled. "Way to see the glass half full."

"Huh?"

Poor Lorenzo. He definitely belonged in the past. "Back to the case. Lorenzo, do you know if a sorcerer needs to touch the person in order to put them into stasis?"

"I've heard they don't."

"That means we don't need to be looking for fingerprints on Gabe's dead body," I mumbled.

"Eww," Gabe said.

Once Nicky translated, Steve tapped his fingers on his desk. "Rihanna, do you think you could ask Hugo and Genevieve to keep an eye on Kitty and Mona? I wouldn't be surprised if one of them tries to skip town. They must know I suspect them of something."

"I'll ask them," I said.

"Thanks. Let me know if you learn anything else."

I realized that I was only nineteen with no legal background, but Steve kind of needed me. He understood if he kept me out of the loop, he probably wouldn't solve this case —or be able to prove any of it.

I stood. "I'll text you what Hugo and Genevieve say."

"Thanks." Once we left, I turned to Nicky. "Do you need to get back or anything?"

"Are you kidding? No. This is too much fun."

I wasn't sure I'd say fun, but I was happy to have had her company. Instead of heading back to the office, we went to the Hex and Bones once more. I waved to Andorra, pointed to the back room, and headed in there.

"I haven't seen Iggy and Bandit yet," Genevieve announced before I'd even asked.

"They might have returned to the office, but we haven't been back. We need another favor."

"Of course. We're always happy to help," she said.

I explained about the need for surveillance. "Steve is worried the guilty party might run."

"That makes sense. I can watch Mona since I doubt she'll put up much of a fight if she tries to get away, and Hugo can have Kitty. She's more likely to run."

I would have switched the assignments. "Why would you watch Mona? She's a powerful sorcerer. I would think Hugo would have better luck than you. No offense."

Genevieve smiled. "None taken. Don't worry, I have my ways. Remember, Mona is quite old and probably a bit arrogant. She won't think anyone will connect her to Gabe's death, assuming she was the one to put the spell on him. Spells can't be traced, and she'll know that."

"True."

Those two disappeared. Good. It would be terrible if our main suspects left town, never to be seen again.

I texted Steve and told him Kitty and Mona wouldn't be going anywhere, thanks to our two gargoyle shifters.

As we were about to leave, Iggy, riding on Bandit's back, came into the back room. I rushed over to him. "Are you hurt? Is that why Bandit is carrying you."

Iggy crawled off. "No. Bandit says I move too slow for him, so he offered me a ride."

"I see."

"So, what happened while we were gone?" He looked around. "And where is Hugo?"

Since Iggy seemed somewhat upset about Hugo's absence, we sat down. I explained what we'd learned and why Hugo and Genevieve weren't there. That took over ten minutes.

"You think Kitty stole the songs and that her mom put Gabe into stasis?" he asked.

"That's our best guess, only we can't prove it. I mean, Lorenzo and Bella heard the band say Sev asked Kitty to grab the songs, but that's hearsay in the legal world. Even if the fingerprints come back as Kitty's, she might make up some reason why her prints were there."

"And you can't prove someone put a curse on someone else, even if they didn't mean to kill Gabe, can you?" Iggy asked.

"No. Any insight as to how we could prove it?" Usually Iggy came up with good suggestions.

He motioned Bandit off to the side. Really? He couldn't speak in front of us?

A few minutes later, they returned. "If the fingerprint stuff doesn't work out, how about if Lorenzo hypnotizes Kitty and tells her to go into the sheriff's department and confess to the theft?" he said.

That wasn't a bad idea. While not legal, no one would be the wiser, I guess. When it came to magic, there were no rules.

"Lorenzo, what do you think?" He'd hypnotized me into doing some silly parlor trick when I was on the cruise.

"When I was alive, I might have succeeded, but now? I don't know. Besides, having Kitty drive while hypnotized could be dangerous. I'm not sure I can control things like I used to."

"Maybe Hugo can do it. Steve doesn't need to know he's behind it." I turned to Bandit. "Remember the woman who killed your host? She hypnotized people to confess."

Bandit moved in front of me. "Yeah, but don't forget that the spell only lasted a few hours."

That would be a problem. "True, and those people claimed they weren't of sound mind at the time of the confession, which was why Steve had to let them go. Darn. Iggy, you had a good suggestion, but I don't think it will work. Any other thoughts? There has to be something we can do."

"Does it have to be legal?" Iggy said.

"We should try to make it legal. Admittedly, even if Mona admitted to putting a spell on Gabe, no court would convict her."

"I have it," Iggy said.

I chuckled. "Do tell."

Iggy moved closer, clearly wanting to have everyone's attention. "Lorenzo could implant a suggestion into the sheriff that would make him think he should arrest Kitty for theft and murder."

"How does that help? He can't prove the murder part."

"I know, but Kitty will be allowed one phone call, right? Isn't that what they do in the movies?"

"Yes." And in real life too.

"And who do you think she'll call?" Iggy asked.

"If I were her, I wouldn't call Sev. I'd call my mom."

"Exactly." He lifted his chest.

I wasn't really understanding his plan. "Walk me through how this helps."

Iggy looked over at Bandit, acting as if I wasn't smart enough to figure things out.

Bandit took a step forward. "Rihanna. Nicky. Here's what Iggy is trying to say. Moms love their kids. We think she'll confess to killing Gabe to spare her daughter from having to stand trial for it."

I wasn't sure all moms would do that. "Mona knows Kitty isn't guilty since she herself is the sorcerer. Why would Mona confess?"

"She's old and probably doesn't have a criminal record. She can plead insanity and get off, whereas they might not go lightly on Kitty who is a thief."

Iggy bobbed his head. "People are put in prison all the time when they are innocent."

"You have been watching too much television," I said.

"But I see your point. I just don't think it will happen that way. Sorry, Gabe, we might never put your killer in prison."

"Maybe not, but at least I'd get closure, assuming my kind can feel that stuff," Gabe said.

"I'm sure you can." He'd experienced depression and guilt as a ghost.

While we'd decided that Kitty and her mom were guilty, it would be nice if one of them could be punished. I didn't care if it was in the human legal system or in the courts run by other witches and warlocks. Glinda had used the latter many times, and justice had been served.

I think the saddest thing—beside Gabe dying—was that Gabe's own band didn't say or do anything to stop this theft since they had played three of Gabe's song at the competition. Sev knew he hadn't written the songs, even if the others didn't.

I was feeling quite sorry for myself for failing to help Gabe when Hugo came in. He rushed over to Iggy who listened intently.

"Wow." Iggy faced me. "Rihanna, you have to text Steve right now and tell him that Kitty is packing her car to leave town."

She might just need a break from all the stress and planned to visit a friend or a relative, but it wasn't up to me to decide that. I pulled out my phone and texted Steve. He could figure out what to do.

Less than two minutes later, a sheriff's car whizzed by with its lights flashing. I turned to Hugo. "Good job, Hugo. How about seeing what Steve will do with Kitty and let us know."

He nodded and disappeared.

I faced Lorenzo. "Why don't you and Bella head on over to the sheriff's office? Perhaps when Steve returns, you can suggest to him that he arrest Kitty for stealing Gabe's song—assuming the fingerprints prove Kitty was in Gabe's house—

and for putting Gabe in a state of stasis, which resulted in his death. If Steve does arrest her for both crimes, Kitty will deny everything—or at least the murder part. However, when she makes her phone call, listen in to the conversation."

Bella clapped—kind of. "This is going to be so cool."

I'm glad she thought so. "Okay. Off you go. Steve, or maybe it's Nash, will be back soon with Kitty."

They disappeared.

"Is there any way we can listen in?" Nicky asked.

"I think it's too late for that. One of the ghosts or shifters will have to fill us in."

"If Steve or Nash arrests Kitty, Hugo and I can listen," Iggy said.

"Me too," Bandit said. "I can cloak myself, remember?"

"True, but you'll both need Hugo or Genevieve to take you inside."

"Whatever," Bandit said, copying Iggy's new favorite phrase.

"Since we have no idea how long this is going to take, Nicky and I are going to head back to the office. It would be very helpful if you two could stay here and let us know when you learn something. Okay?"

"Yes, ma'am," Iggy said.

That stopped me in my tracks. I couldn't recall Iggy ever calling me ma'am in his life.

Nicky and I left. "Do you really think Steve can get Kitty to confess?"

"If he receives confirmation about the fingerprints, he'll try. If they don't match Kitty's, he won't hold her, and we'll be back to square one."

"That stinks," she said.

"Tell me about it."

We left, and once back in the office, I fixed us some tea and some snacks. Nicky and I were tossing out ideas when Bella appeared in the office.

"You won't believe it," she said.

From her excited state, something good had happened. "Do tell."

"I don't know where to begin."

"How about telling us if Steve arrested Kitty or not?"

"He did."

I waited for some details, but maybe she was trying to be dramatic. "What did Kitty say? Or Steve for that matter?"

"Steve received the fingerprint information from the sheriff where Gabe lived. They were a match. Her fingerprints were all over the books and the computer as we suspected."

"That's great, though I'm kind of surprised she didn't think to wear gloves," I said.

"Not all thieves are smart."

"True. Go on."

"When Steve told her that her fingerprints were found in Gabe's house, as well as her fox hair on the floor, she folded. Kitty said she was in Gabe's place looking for his new songs. I have to say the crying jag was impressive."

"Meaning you didn't believe her?"

"Exactly. It was so fake. She admitted that she stole the songs because she was mad that Gabe had lost her mom money."

"Kitty admitted that Mona was her mother?" I asked.

"Yes, but only after Steve, or maybe it was Nash, said they knew."

"Did Lorenzo do his mind meld thing?" Nicky asked.

I chuckled at her description. "You mean did he manage to implant the idea in Steve's mind that he should arrest Kitty for murder despite having no proof?"

Bella grinned. "He did. Lorenzo was amazing. It took a few tries for him to get it right, but eventually he did."

"Then what? Did Kitty make a phone call?"

Just then Lorenzo came in. "Bella, you're stealing my thunder."

I laughed. "Lorenzo, you'll get all the credit if this works. I assume Gabe is still at the jail watching her?"

"Yes, as is Hugo. Genevieve is still with Mona. I did a quick stop at that occult store and gave Iggy and Bandit the rundown about what was happening. Iggy wanted to wait for Hugo to get back before he returned here."

"That's Iggy for you." I raised my eyebrows, hoping Lorenzo would tell me some other news, but he didn't. "Did Kitty make her one call?"

"Not yet, but Gabe said he'd listen in if and when she did."

Genevieve would listen on Mona's end. Ugh. So close yet so far. "Thank you." I sipped my tea. "And now we wait."

chapter
nineteen

SINCE I DIDN'T WANT to miss any updates from Hugo, Gabe, Genevieve, or the sheriff, I ordered food from the Tiki Hut grill to be delivered.

No sooner had the food arrived than Hugo teleported in with Iggy.

Yes! "I trust you two have news?"

"We do," Iggy said. "Steve isn't good at extracting information from people, so Hugo had to help."

"You know we can't use what Hugo found out in court, right?"

"I know the rule. Sheesh. While Kitty admitted to stealing Gabe's songs, she denied killing Gabe. I'm sure she'll do time for the theft at least."

"I'm glad you're so sure. Let's hope you're selected for the jury."

He faced Hugo. "She's a laugh a minute, isn't she?"

I swear Hugo was fighting a smile.

"Did Kitty admit that her mom was the one to put the spell on Gabe?" I asked. "If she did, it would make Kitty an accessory to the crime, though I'm no lawyer."

Hugo communicated with Iggy telepathically—a skill I'd love to have.

"No. She wouldn't say," Iggy translated.

"Anything else?" I asked.

Iggy faced me. "While Kitty didn't put Gabe in stasis, when she learned Gabe was *really* dead, she panicked."

"If she used the word *really*, it implied she knew about the stasis," Nicky said.

"Seems like it. Maybe that's why there were fox prints outside of the barn. She was checking on his status. When Kitty returned and found him gone, I can see why she'd be upset. Hugo, what did Kitty do that indicated she panicked?"

Iggy consulted Hugo again and then faced us. "She covered up the crime—or so she thought—by erasing DMan's memory of him having heard the song that Gabe sang to him. When Steve asked her about erasing the songs on Gabe's phone, she denied it."

"The killer—Mona—would have done that. Or at least that seems the most likely scenario."

"Do you think Mona planned to take Gabe out of stasis?" Nicky asked me.

"Initially? That would be my guess. Otherwise, why put him into stasis in the first place—assuming she knew how to kill a person? We may never know if Mona would have changed her mind if we hadn't found Gabe."

"I bet she would have wanted him dead when she realized that if she removed the stasis spell, Gabe would have asked to be in the band. It wouldn't take Gabe long to realize they'd stolen his songs."

This was becoming complicated. "Tell me if I have this right. Rod is guilty of telling his band members that Gabe had new songs, though he might not have been aware that the ones Sev said he'd written actually came from Gabe."

"Hugo said that Steve didn't ask her about how she knew about the new songs or how anyone knew," Iggy announced.

"What about that Steely Contreau guy?" Nicky asked. "Was he involved?"

Hugo shrugged.

"It seems as if Sev was the main instigator once he found out that Gabe had written new songs." I said.

"So, did we solve the case?" Iggy asked.

"Partially. We know that Carla told Rod that Gabe had written new songs and that Rob told Sev about it. DMan might be guilty, but I don't know of what. As for who put Gabe into stasis, the only one capable is Mona."

"Do you think she'll confess though?" Nicky asked.

"If I were a psychic, I might know, but I'm not, so I don't." I looked over at Hugo. "Genevieve is watching Mona. She'll be there when Mona receives the phone call from her daughter—assuming Kitty calls her. Hugo, can you find out—"

"Where did he go?" Nicky asked.

"Hugo is often one step ahead of me. He's going to find Genevieve and ask her about the phone call. We should find out soon enough what happened."

"I'd like to be a fly on the wall when that goes down," Iggy said.

"If Hugo comes back, ask him to take you to the sheriff's department. You can be our eyes and ears," I suggested.

"Okay."

He didn't sound all that excited. "What's wrong?"

"You have Gabe, Lorenzo, Bella, Genevieve, and Hugo who can spy whenever you want them to. When I help Glinda, there's just me and Hugo. And sometimes Genevieve."

I had to take a second to decode what he was really saying. "Just because we have more helpers doesn't make you any less important."

"I guess. Got any lettuce?"

I chuckled. "I'll fix you a plate." I nodded to the chicken wings. "Nicky, do you want me to warm this up? It's been sitting for a bit."

Nicky touched a corner. "Nope. It's good."

I went into the kitchen for food for Iggy. Once I fixed a plate, I carried it out and placed it on the coffee table. "Here you go."

"Thanks." He took two bites. "I bet Mona confesses since she has to know she won't be convicted. She never touched the body."

"I think she'll think there are no laws against performing a spell. People who shoot someone don't touch the body, and they are guilty."

Iggy looked off to the side. "Oh, yeah. There is that."

I plopped down on the sofa and picked up a wing. The first bite was divine, and I moaned. "When I'm in the middle of trying to solve a crime, it's hard to remember to eat."

Nicky chuckled. "I'm the same way when I take pictures. I become lost in my own little world."

"So true."

We'd finished when Genevieve appeared. "Quick. Gabe needs Bella and Lorenzo's help."

Both of them moved closer to Genevieve. "What can we do?" Bella asked.

"After Mona received a phone call from her daughter, she drove to the sheriff's office where she admitted that she was the one to put Gabe into stasis."

Iggy's plan worked! "Did she say why she confessed?" I asked.

"I don't know. Let me finish."

"Okay." Genevieve seemed to be in a big hurry.

"Mona said a few days after she put Gabe into stasis, she

returned to the farm house to return him to his living state only to find his body was gone."

"His body was gone, but what is Steve going to do about her confession? There are no laws that deal with the occult or spells or anything—unless he plans to have her tried in the *other* court of law." We had an occult court system on the other side of the state that no one but local people of magic knew about.

"Does it matter if she's willing to sign a confession that says she attempted to kill Gabe?" Genevieve asked.

"Attempted to kill him? What happened to her comment that she just put him into stasis?" I asked.

She waved a hand. "There are reasons why, but she claimed she planned to take Gabe out of stasis until Sev claimed the songs Kitty stole were his. Then she changed her mind to protect her daughter. At least I think that was what she said. I don't know. She was babbling a lot."

"Did she say why she put Gabe into stasis in the first place?" Surely, Steve asked her that.

"Yes, because Kitty worried that Gabe would hear about the band contest and want part of the action, giving less money to each person should they win," she said. "Once more, Mona was trying to help her daughter."

That was kind of sweet, but putting a spell on Gabe to help Kitty wasn't the answer. "They weren't going to win without him, and some of the band members must have realized that. Or maybe Mona really wanted Gabe dead because he lost her money and used this stasis thing as a test to see if she could live with herself if he died."

Iggy faced me. "If we'd never found Gabe, would he still be alive today?"

"That's a great question. I don't know. Only Lorenzo can answer that—or Mona—though if Gabe is a vampire, I'm betting he would be alive today."

Iggy dropped onto his stomach. "I'm sorry I have such good eyes. If I hadn't seen Gabe, he might have lived."

"Iggy, when I went inside to take pictures, I would have seen him. Besides, I think kids visited the farmhouse too."

"Maybe."

Bella flew between me and Genevieve. It was a passive aggressive move, but I couldn't blame her. I should have saved my questions until later.

"You said Gabe needed our help?" Bella asked.

"Yes. Sorry. I was distracted telling the story. Gabe is floating all around Mona saying he'll haunt her until the end of time, both in this life and afterward, if she doesn't make amends—and by amends he means she has to confess to everything."

"So that was why she admitted her guilt," I mumbled.

Genevieve ignored my comment. "I was hoping you two could support his efforts. If Mona sees the three of you, she might sign instantly, hoping that the courts will show her leniency."

"I don't imagine someone with her power would want to be haunted from now through eternity. That was brilliant on Gabe's part." Bella raised her hands over her head in a victory pose, her voodoo doll dangling from her fingers.

I didn't have the heart to ask if it bothered her that she couldn't put it down.

Bella looked over at Lorenzo, nodded, and then floated through the office wall. Lorenzo followed.

I expected Genevieve to go, too, but she didn't. "Would you ladies, and gentlemen, like a front row seat to the chaos?"

"Yes!" This would be so cool. I didn't even ask Iggy if he wanted to go. I picked him up and placed him on my shoulder.

"How is this going to work?" Nicky asked.

I nodded to Genevieve who explained it. "I touch your

shoulder, and we'll teleport to the sheriff's conference room. Here's the thing. While no one can see us, they can hear us, so no talking."

"That will be hard," Nicky said.

I smiled. "You can do it."

"Okay."

One second we were in the Pink Iguana Sleuth's office and the next we were in the conference room. Steve, Hugo, our ghost contingent, and Mona were there. I assumed Kitty was in one of the holding cells and that Nash was still watching her. Foxes were small and could probably squeeze through the bars.

Genevieve moved us to the far end of the room, away from any chairs, just in case someone shoved back their seat and accidentally hit us.

Gabe, and now Bella and Lorenzo were circling Mona. She would glance their way on occasion, but since Steve was speaking, she tried to listen to him. Too bad he had no idea what was going on.

Gabe flew in front of her face. "I warned you about Cloud 9, Mona. You were the one who invested your money. You were greedy. I showed you safer options."

She looked up at him. "I know. I'm sorry."

"Mona?" Steve asked.

I was curious to see if she mentioned there were ghosts in the room. Normally, it would help with a plea of insanity, but Steve wouldn't buy it. He believed ghosts existed, even if he couldn't see them. If she went before her peers, she couldn't use that excuse either.

"Yes?"

"Is something wrong?" he asked.

"No." She wove her hands together. "I think I'm ready to sign my confession."

"Are you sure?"

"Yes. I'm willing to have my peers judge me."

Steve moved the paper in front of her, and when she signed, the relief that went through me was immense. Whether Mona would ever see a prison cell was anyone's guess, but at least we'd figured out who killed Gabe.

He grinned, motioned for Bella and Lorenzo to follow him, and then went through the office to the outside. I tapped Genevieve's shoulder to indicate we'd seen enough.

When we appeared in the office, all three ghosts were there. I didn't know where Hugo was, but he might have decided to stay around to make sure Mona didn't try to put a curse on Steve or something.

"Congratulations," I announced to the happy ghosts.

"Rihanna, I don't know what to say. I'm upset that someone I dated would turn on me like that, but I'm happy Kitty will be punished," Gabe said.

"What about your songs?" I asked.

He shrugged. "Someone might as well enjoy listening to them. I can't exactly make recordings anymore."

Poor Gabe.

Lorenzo floated in front of Gabe. "About that. I took a quick trip to New Orleans to ask about something I thought existed."

"What are you talking about?"

"I know of a *ghost* band, for lack of a better term, that would love to have you join them."

"That is so cool," Nicky said.

I couldn't picture how that would work. "Without any substance to his body, how can he play?" I asked Lorenzo.

He tapped the stake in his chest. Clearly, it had no effect on him. "It's like what you people now call karaoke. True, only other ghosts can hear him, but it's still cool. My family's club has lounges where humans go to sing. Since no one can see you—or probably not many—you can sing along."

"But I can't sing my own songs."

I had an idea. "You might be able to convince someone to play your song while you sing it. They'd have to be able to see you, of course, but it is New Orleans. Since that town has a lot of voodoo people, they probably have witches and warlocks too."

"I bet my grandmother can find someone for you," Bella said.

Gabe smiled. "Thanks for the offer. I'd love to give it a go."

"My pleasure," Lorenzo said.

Gabe inhaled. "There is one more thing to take care of."

"What's that?"

"It's about my house and my belongings. I have a will, but unfortunately, I left my possessions to the band. I wrote it in a weak moment. I'd like to redo it."

Did he remember he couldn't write or speak with his attorney? "How do you plan on doing that?" I asked.

"I don't know. That's the problem. Could I dictate what I want to you, and you could type it up and give it my attorney?"

"I could, but I don't think it would be legal. Your lawyer has your original, and he would think I just made it up, especially since you can't sign the document."

Bella moved in front. "I have an idea."

"What is it?" I asked.

"I'm not sure if I ever mentioned it, but I have a talent or two that I believe I still possess."

That was news. "What would that be?"

"I'd have to make a quick trip to New Orleans for one of my grandmother's spells, but if it works, I should be able to take Gabe's original will and replace it with a new one. The signature, date, letterhead, everything, would be the same. Just the contents would be different."

"Wow. That is some skill. And a scary one at that." No

telling what she could change. A confession, perhaps? Or worse, a Bill from Congress.

"Are you ready to write up my Last Will and Testament?" he asked me.

"Let's do it."

It took less than an hour for me to type up Gabe's new will. By the time we finished, Bella had returned from New Orleans with the spell she needed.

"Gabe, you'll need to show me where your lawyer's office is."

"I can do that."

"Guys, maybe you should have Genevieve or Hugo go with you in case you need to use a computer or open a drawer," I said.

"Good idea." And then they were gone.

"Do you think it will work?" Iggy asked.

"If Bella is involved, I bet she'll make it work."

As soon as they left, I texted Elliot with the good news about who'd killed Gabe. I wasn't sure he'd be happy, but he needed to know Mona wouldn't be stopping by anytime soon.

chapter
twenty

THREE DAYS LATER, Glinda and Jaxson returned home from their camping trip, and I was so happy to see them—as was Iggy, though he wouldn't tell them that .

After many hugs and making sure Iggy was good, Glinda asked how my week went.

"I solved a murder," Iggy announced before I had the chance to answer my cousin.

"You did?" Glinda asked. "All by yourself?"

"You are silly. No. I had help." Iggy proceeded to give her some of the details.

Glinda turned to me. "How about Jaxson and I clean up and meet you at the Tiki Hut Grill in an hour? I want to hear everything. It was a long drive, and I'd like to change." She faced Iggy. "I also I want to hear how you and Bandit saved the day."

"And Hugo, as well as Bella, Lorenzo, and the rest of the people."

She smiled. "Sounds great."

Iggy headed toward the door. "Where are you going?" Glinda asked.

"To tell Bandit you're back."

I wasn't sure why he'd care, but they did seem to enjoy each other's company.

Once all three were gone, I changed. I looked around my room, wondering if any of the ghosts were hiding, ready to jump out at me. Ever since Bella died, I'd grown attached to having her and Lorenzo come and go. I actually liked each of the ghosts we'd interacted with too.

I couldn't help but wonder if I would see them again, but then I told myself that if any other ghosts learned Bella and Lorenzo had contacts with ghost-seeing people in the real world, they'd want to have me try to solve their murders.

At first, I liked the idea, until I realized some of the ghosts could be dangerous. The last thing I needed was to have a serial killer request I figure out who killed him.

After I finished straightening up, I headed out to the Tiki Hut Grill. I was anxious to hear all about Glinda and Jaxson's adventure too. When I walked in, both were at the counter talking with Aunt Fern.

I went over to say hello, and after we chatted a bit, Aunt Fern walked us to our table. "Glinda, once you're rested, please stop by and tell me all about your trip."

"I will."

We placed our order, and then I leaned back in my seat. "So how was it?"

Glinda told me that she and Jaxson had been living in their tent about three days when she told him if she didn't have a hot shower, she'd go crazy. Naturally, her fiancé gave in.

"Once you decided the camping life wasn't for you, what did you do?" I asked. They'd stayed on vacation the whole week.

"I rented a hotel room." Jaxson reached over and clasped Glinda's hand. "She was willing to take small day hikes and that worked for me."

"How was the mountain climbing?" I asked. I cheated and

peeked into Glinda's thoughts to learn she actually had a good time.

"Hard on the body, but the beauty of the streams and forests was something I'll never forget. Do I want to go back next month? Probably not, but I won't say never."

Jaxson and I both laughed.

"Iggy mentioned something about Gabe altering his will after his death? Did that work?" Glinda asked.

"It did, though when his attorney called me, I feared I'd been caught doing something illegal."

Jaxson half smiled. "Be honest. Changing the will of a dead person is illegal."

"I know, but Gabe insisted. I figured if magic was involved, no one could prove anything."

Jaxson held up a hand. "I get it. Go on. Who did he leave his money to?"

"He donated some of his possessions to Witch's Cove High School to support music appreciation and some to the Boys and Girls club in his town."

"That is so sweet," Glinda said. "I wish I'd been here to meet him."

"Me too. Gabe was a great guy. I'd be remiss if I didn't mention he left me a generous stipend for solving his murder."

"How thoughtful."

"He wanted to give me more, but I told him no, so he gave the remainder to Nicky. She's been wanting a new camera for a long time and now she could finally afford one."

"I love it when cases wrap up so nicely," Glinda said.

"I agree."

"I know it's only been a few days, but did Steve say what would happen to Kitty and Mona?" Jaxson asked.

"Kitty will stand trial in our courts for stealing Gabe's songs."

"And her mom?" Glinda asked.

"She will be tried in our special court for people like her. If they believe she planned to bring Gabe out of his stasis, they might go easy on her, but I hope not. Gabe died. We'll have to see."

"While Glinda and I had a very interesting time on our trip, clearly it was bad timing on our part. I would have liked to have been here. It sounds like it was a great case."

"It was," I said.

"You said Lorenzo believed Gabe was vampire. Did you ever find any confirmation to that fact?" Glinda asked.

"Not really, but Lorenzo is sure that only a vampire can be put into statis, so I'd say yes."

"I hope he's okay with it."

"I think so." Or at least Gabe seemed to accept his fate.

"Were you sad to say goodbye to Bella and Lorenzo?" Glinda asked.

I chuckled. "You know, I was. They've grown on me, but I wouldn't mind a few months of relaxation. I have no doubt that some emergency will require a human to intervene, and they'll return. Bella seems to have developed quite the heart. I think she believes it's her duty to help all those in need—or should I say all ghosts who've died under strange circumstances."

"I really should visit Levy to see if that woman you met, Melissa was it, could put a spell on us so we can see all ghosts. I would love to interact with those two."

I smiled. "Be careful what you wish for."

I hope you enjoyed another Rihanna adventure with Gabe and our sleuthing ghosts. If you want to learn what's next, sign up for my Cozy Mystery newsletter.

THE END

about the author

Love it HOT and STEAMY? Sign up for my newsletter and receive MONTANA DESIRE for FREE. <u>Click here</u>

OR Are you a fan of quirky PARANORMAL COZY MYSTERIES? Sign up for this newsletter. <u>Click Here</u>

Not only do I love to read, write, and dream, I'm an extrovert. I enjoy being around people and am always trying to understand what makes them tick. Not only must my romance books have a happily ever after, I need characters I can relate to. My men are wonderful, dynamic, smart, strong, and the best lovers in the world (of course).

My Paranormal Cozy Mysteries are where I let my imagination run wild with witches and a talking pink iguana who believes he's a real sleuth.

I believe I am the luckiest woman. I do what I love and I have a wonderful, supportive husband, who happens to be hot!

Fun facts about me

(1) I'm a math nerd who loves spreadsheets. Give me numbers and I'll find a pattern.

(2) I live on a Costa Rica beach!

(3) I also like to exercise. Yes, I know I'm odd.

I love hearing from readers either on FB or via email (hint, hint).

Social Media Sites

Website: www.velladay.com
    FB: www.facebook.com/vella.day.90
    Twitter: velladay4
    Gmail: velladayauthor@gmail.com

also by vella day

<u>A WITCH'S COVE MYSTERY</u> (Paranormal Cozy Mystery)

PINK Is The New Black (book 1)

A PINK Potion Gone Wrong (book 2)

The Mystery of the PINK Aura (book 3)

Box Set (books 1-3)

Sleuthing In The PINK (book 4)

Not in The PINK (book 5)

Gone in the PINK of an Eye (book 6)

Box Set (books 4-6)

The PINK Pumpkin Party (book 7)

Mistletoe with a PINK Bow (book 8)

The Magical PINK Pendant (book 9)

The Poisoned PINK Punch (book 10)

PINK Smoke and Mirrors (book 11)

Broomsticks and PINK Gumdrops (book 12)

Knotted Up In PINK Yarn (book 13)

Ghosts and PINK Candles (book 14)

Pilfering The PINK Pearls (book 15)

The Case of The Stolen PINK Tombstone (book 16)

The PINK Christmas Cookie Caper (book 17)

PINK Moon Rising (book 18)

<u>A VOODOO & VAMPIRE MYSTERY</u> (a spinoff of A Witch's Cove Mystery)

Call Me Ghostly(Book 1)

Better Late Than Staked (Book 2)

Ghosts Just Want To Have Fun (Book 3)

SILVER LAKE SERIES (3 OF THEM)

(1). **<u>HIDDEN REALMS OF SILVER LAKE</u>** (Paranormal Romance)

Awakened By Flames (book 1)

Seduced By Flames (book 2)

Kissed By Flames (book 3)

Destiny In Flames (book 4)

Box Set (books 1-4)

Passionate Flames (book 5)

Ignited By Flames (book 6)

Touched By Flames (book 7)

Box Set (books 5-7)

Bound By Flames (book 8)

Fueled By Flames (book 9)

Scorched By Flames (book 10)

(2). **<u>FOUR SISTERS OF FATE: HIDDEN REALMS OF SILVER LAKE</u>** (Paranormal Romance)

Poppy (book 1)

Primrose (book 2)

Acacia (book 3)

Magnolia (book 4)

Box Set (books 1-4)

Jace (book 5)

Tanner (book 6)

(3). WERES AND WITCHES OF SILVER LAKE (Paranormal Romance)

A Magical Shift (book 1)

Catching Her Bear (book 2)

Surge of Magic (book 3)

The Bear's Forbidden Wolf (book 4)

Her Reluctant Bear (book 5)

Freeing His Tiger (book 6)

Protecting His Wolf (book 7)

Waking His Bear (book 8)

Melting Her Wolf's Heart (book 9)

Her Wolf's Guarded Heart (book 10)

His Rogue Bear (book 11)

Box Set (books 1-4)

Box Set (books 5-8)

Reawakening Their Bears (book 12)

OTHER PARANORMAL SERIES

PACK WARS (Paranormal Romance)

Training Their Mate (book 1)

Claiming Their Mate (book 2)

Rescuing Their Virgin Mate (book 3)

Box Set (books 1-3)

Loving Their Vixen Mate (book 4)

Fighting For Their Mate (book 5)

Enticing Their Mate (book 6)

Their Huntress Mate (book 7)

Box Set (books 1-4)

HIDDEN HILLS SHIFTERS (Paranormal Romance)

An Unexpected Diversion (book 1)

Bare Instincts (book 2)

Shifting Destinies (book 3)

Embracing Fate (book 4)

Promises Unbroken (book 5)

Bare 'N Dirty (book 6)

Hidden Hills Shifters Complete Box Set (books 1-6)

CONTEMPORARY SERIES

MONTANA PROMISES (Full length contemporary Romance)

Promises of Mercy (book 1)

Foundations For Three (book 2)

Montana Fire (book 3)

Montana Promises Box Set (books 1-3)

Hart To Hart (Book 4)

Burning Seduction (Book 5)

Montana Promises Complete Box Set (books 1-5)

ROCK HARD, MONTANA (contemporary romance novellas)

Montana Desire (book 1)

Awakening Passions (book 2)

PLEDGED TO PROTECT (contemporary romantic suspense)

From Panic To Passion (book 1)

From Danger To Desire (book 2)

From Terror To Temptation (book 3)

Pledged To Protect Box Set (books 1-3)

BURIED SERIES (contemporary romantic suspense)

Buried Alive (book 1)

Buried Secrets (book 2)

Buried Deep (book 3)

The Buried Series Complete Box Set (books 1-3)

A NASH MYSTERY (Contemporary Romance)

Sidearms and Silk(book 1)

Black Ops and Lingerie(book 2)

A Nash Mystery Box Set (books 1-2)

STARTER SETS (Romance)

Contemporary

Paranormal